MW01528919

MURDER IN MISSOULA

MURDER IN MISSOULA
Published by Château Noir Publishing
Copyright © 2014 by Laurence Giliotti
All rights reserved.

MURDER IN MISSOULA is a work of fiction. All incidents, dialogue,
and characters are products of the author's imagination.
In all respects any resemblance between the characters and persons
living or dead is coincidental.

ISBN: Print: 978-0-9909266-2-7
ISBN: ebook: 978-0-9909266-3-4

Cover design by Rebecca Swift

Château Noir Publishing, P.O. Box 19110,
Boulder, Colorado 80308, U.S.A.

Printed in the United States of America

Dedicated to

The Innocent Victims of Evil

MURDER IN MISSOULA

LAURENCE GILIOTTI

Château Noir Publishing

ONE

The body was a few feet below him in a depression at the base of a large tree. The undulating terrain kept the decaying remains hidden from any vantage point other than the knoll on which he was standing.

FBI special agent Leonard Pandori shifted his weight onto his left leg. The leg he referred to as his "good leg." He leaned heavily on his walking stick. The climb down from the road had left him winded, his muscles shaking from the effort.

"You all right?" Undersheriff Doug Martin asked.

"Fine, just getting my sea legs." Pandori looked back toward the road where a deputy was interviewing a man and a young boy. "Who found the body?"

"The boy. They were walking along the creek, looking for a spot to build a tree stand. The father sent the kid up the hill to check out this tree. When the kid climbed up and looked around, he spotted this necklace." Martin pulled a plastic evidence bag from his pocket. "It wasn't until he climbed down to get it that he saw the body."

Pandori looked at the silver and turquoise of the Navaho squash blossom necklace. He had seen it a hundred times before on the flyers that had been posted all over the county six months ago.

Martin put the bag back into his pocket. "Sorry to drag you out so early on a Saturday, but once I saw the necklace, I figured I better give you a call. We can't be certain, but I'm willing to bet we're looking at Candice Wilson."

Except for a few training seminars, nothing in Pandori's twenty-five years with the FBI prepared him to run a homicide investigation. Martin supervised all of the county's investigation teams. Pandori was grateful to have him in charge.

"I called for Bennigan to bring out his bloodhound, Duke," Martin said.

"Looks like the body has been here quite a while. You think a dog will be of any use?"

"You never know. My bet is someone had to bring her down from the road. Maybe the killer comes back to visit with her on sunny afternoons. There's a scarf around her neck that looks fairly new. It could be a recent addition to the scene. Bennigan can use it as a scent article to give the dog something to go on. If there's a scent of the killer on it, maybe Duke will find it."

"How reliable is the dog?"

"We'll see. If he does get a scent, it will probably just go as far as the road. The killer had to use a car."

"I read somewhere that bloodhounds could follow the scent of a vehicle."

"As far as I know, that kind of thing happens only in fiction, not in the real world."

"We should probably get some photos from up in the tree to show the view from where the boy spotted the necklace," Pandori said.

"The crime scene unit will be here in about twenty minutes. We can go back up to my car. I've got a thermos of hot coffee, unless you want to wait here and—"

"Coffee sounds good." Pandori patted his coat pockets. "Must have left my cell phone in the car. Can I use yours?"

"There's no service until you get back up to the road."

They started to climb the steep hillside, Undersheriff Martin moving slowly to allow Pandori to keep pace.

"I should have called to cancel my breakfast date before I left the house." Pandori breath became irregular as he struggled with the effort.

Martin stopped and extended a hand to support his trailing companion. "Your wife leaves town and you already have a date lined up?"

"It's an old friend, Joe Nicoletti. He's a—"

"I remember him, the DEA agent... He was here, visiting you last spring, when Candice Wilson went missing."

"Yeah, that's right." Pandori used the leverage of Martin's arm to take the lead. "Now he's back and so is she." He pointed the cane toward the corpse.

"Sanchez is gonna be pissed."

"What?" Pandori turned to see a grin spread across Martin's face.

"Lieutenant Sanchez—She was really hot for your pal—swore if she ever saw him again she'd take him home for dinner, even if she had to cuff him."

"I'll warn him."

"No need, she's on leave, visiting family in Salt Lake City." Martin signaled a deputy to grab hold of Pandori and pull him up onto the road.

"Well, Lt. Sanchez may get her chance if I can convince Nicoletti to take a job at the university. Since he retired he's—"

"Retired? I thought he was a younger guy."

"You mean not as old and decrepit as me?"

"Well, I didn't mean it that way, but since you mentioned it..."

"Get the coffee. I've got a call to make, then let's focus on Candice Wilson."

TWO

Charles Durbin depended on sunny Saturday mornings. They were his source of joy, providing inspiration for his darker fantasies.

While meticulously grooming Mrs. Coulter's brown-and-white cocker spaniel, Durbin dreamed of his special time with Marie-Justine. He glanced at the clock—9:30, right on schedule. Mrs. Coulter promised to pick up her little darling at 9:45 sharp. He had cautioned her, "Now don't be late, dear."

Durbin fluffed the cocker's back with the dryer, supporting the lustrous fur with his sinewy fingers. The muscles of his right forearm bulged against the veins as he rhythmically moved the dryer side to side. Satisfied with the results, he shut the dryer off, returned it to the stainless steel holder at the end of the grooming table, and brushed the freshly cleaned fur one last time. He carried the dog to a wooden pen near the front door. He filled a small aluminum bowl with water and set it inside the pen, then put the grooming tools in the sterilizer, swept, and vacuumed the wooden floor.

"Mommy should be along any minute," he said to the dog.

In the kitchen at the rear of the house, he poured a cup of tea and turned on the stereo. Puccini's romantic visions drifted through the old house. Durbin hummed, knowing that he was soon to be with his Marie-Justine, a woman who would appreciate his music and be thrilled to find that they both drank the same brand of tea. He even had the same style teacups she preferred. What a wonderful coincidence.

Mrs. Coulter was late.

He stalked into the grooming area at the front of the house and stared at the dog. "I've got places to go. Where the hell is that senile, old bitch?"

He looked at Mrs. Coulter's red leather leash among the row of black nylon leads hanging on wooden pegs in the front entry.

The dog lowered his ears and submissively tucked its tail.

Durbin moved toward the dog. He wanted to attach the little beggar to the red leather leash, drag him outside, and swing him through the air like a bolo, smashing his perky little skull onto the front walk. That would teach her to be on time.

Durbin calmed himself and walked back to the kitchen. No sense in letting that genie out of the bottle, he thought. He didn't want any unpleasantness to interrupt his new life in Montana. He had been careless in Colorado and leaving there had saddened him. Living in Colorado Springs had been comfortable, and his home there had been more charming than the rambling Victorian he now occupied. But Missoula was safe for now, as long as he was careful and under control.

He didn't like the idea of playing cat and mouse with detectives. He didn't like the police. Toying with them always ended badly for his kind. That was why he had decided to leave Colorado. It had been a preemptive move. They were not looking in his direction, but one cannot be too careful when eluding bloodhounds.

Fortunately, the police do not have the dedication of the hound and are easily sidetracked with new priorities. By now, his little Colorado adventures were "old news." He had nothing to fear from his past and was free to renew his strength in the Saturday morning light of western Montana.

At ease in his new surroundings, his future was promising. He had taken over the house and pet grooming business from an elderly couple for a few thousand dollars down and a promise to pay, secured by a handshake.

Since then things had gone well, and as long as he remained cautious, they would stay that way. He was not some crazed, frenzy-driven maniac hunting for isolated prostitutes or forgotten old women living alone. Those temptations were everywhere, and their abundance made the hunter careless, wasteful, like a grizzly standing in a river teaming with salmon, snatching the writhing silver bodies teeth and claw, tearing into the pink flesh for a greedy bite, then tossing the gasping carcass onto the riverbank as the glutton's attention is drawn to the next victim.

That behavior was the downfall of his kindred spirits. Durbin had read of their exploits in books and newspapers that chronicled their foolish mistakes, compounding one on top of another as they deteriorated in their selectivity and technique. They were savage bears, believing only in their own omnipotence, oblivious to their transformation from noble hunters into pathetic peasant harvesters. In each and every case, their downward spiral was predictable. The police, unable to stop the killings, waited, hoping the predator would eventually provide a trail leading back to his cave. The greater the feeding frenzies, the clearer the trail.

Durbin rinsed the teacup and set it on the drain board under the yellow-and-white café curtains fluttering above the sink. He inhaled the cool breeze. He was not concerned with the plight of the others. They were Philistines, settling for whatever mongrels the gods might toss them. He was different. His women were special— exotic and intelligent; they had elegance and style and were the rare, best of breed. He was an aristocrat with aristocratic taste.

Sensing Mrs. Coulter's approach, he went to the front door. "Here's your little treasure," he said as he led the dog out on the red leather leash.

"I'm so sorry to be late, Charles. I know you have an appointment."

"Don't worry yourself for a moment, Mrs. Coulter. I have plenty of time."

"Well, I know how you young people are. So busy, so impatient. I hope your young lady appreciates what a catch you are." She turned and walked toward her car, the cocker trying to run ahead, pulling, straining at the lead to flee the fear of being nothing more than helpless prey.

Durbin went upstairs to his bedroom. Unbuttoning his shirt, he watched from the front window as Mrs. Coulter drove away. He had to hurry. He was too late to meet Marie-Justine at her home. He would have to catch up with her at the café. But first, he must shower and put on fresh clothes. He never carried the scent of business to the table of pleasure.

THREE

Across the river, the October sun dappled the roof of a yellow-and-white cottage nestled amid the mature landscaping of the university section of Missoula. Inside, Marie-Justine sipped a cup of tea and looked at the empty FedEx envelope. Her Los Angeles attorney had addressed it in her maiden name, Marie-Justine Junot.

She had not decided if she was going to use her maiden name after the divorce. For now, she was listed in the Genetic Sciences section of the University of Montana Faculty Directory as Professor Marie-Justine Cantrell, PhD. The divorce proceedings had been dragging on for two years, but it had been amicable. Her soon-to-be ex-husband, Dr. Richard Cantrell, had been cautious but fair.

She spread the pages of the final settlement on the kitchen table, initialed and dated the bottom of each page, signed the last, and slid them into the return envelope.

Could this be all there was to it, after all this time?

She would drop it in the FedEx box on campus before meeting Anne for their regular Saturday morning coffee. After years of listening to the late-night calls and reading Marie-Justine's sad, painful letters detailing the frustration of her unhappy marriage, Anne would also be relieved that it was finally over.

Marie-Justine had other news for Anne. Last night, the silent stranger had once more come to her in a dream. For months in a recurring dream, she felt herself running through a dark, damp forest, hunted by an unseen force. Running, gasping for air, trying to scream, but no sound came. Hands reached at her from the darkness. She stumbled between thorn bushes and vines that alternately tore and pulled at her flesh.

Just when she felt she could breathe no more, a stranger would appear, running at her side. He would wrap her in his muscular arms and carry her into a field bathed in moonlight. Then, as suddenly as he had appeared, the stranger would be gone, leaving her alone yet at peace.

Last night, the dream was different.

Last night, there was no terror. She had held the stranger's hand, and they walked on a mist-covered hillside. She spoke to him in French. He never replied, but she could see his eyes and knew his thoughts. Under the trees, on a bed of soft, silver pine boughs, they made love, and when she awoke, she still felt his warmth around her.

She pressed the teacup against her full lips. How odd, she thought, that her dream conversations were always in her native French. She had learned English as a child and had spoken it almost exclusively for the last thirty years. Now, except for overseas phone conversations with her father and grandfather and occasional confidential remarks to Anne when in the company of others, she never spoke French. In fact, she was sure she no longer even thought in French. But in her dreams...

Marie-Justine looked for her cell phone. She had left it on the patio. She picked up the house phone. Anne would have a simple, logical explanation for last night's dream, rejecting any prophetic qualities and attributing it solely to the pressure and final release of the divorce.

The line was busy.

Marie-Justine set the teacup in the sink and reached through the yellow-and-white café curtains to close the window.

She crossed the house and stepped onto the flagstone patio. Her thick, chestnut-colored hair was still damp from the shower. On the patio she brushed it against the breeze. The cool strands whisked into the warm sunlight and fell across her shoulders, heightening her senses. She couldn't remember the last time she had been so aware of her life and the joy of it. Maybe Anne was right and her sense of foreboding had been tied to the divorce.

Eight years of marriage, each more difficult than its predecessor, followed by two years of legal separation, were finally at an end. She was happy. She was free. Free of a childhood infatuation mistaken for love, a mistake that imprisoned the woman she had become.

She took the cell phone from the patio table and dialed Anne's number again.

"What?"

"You sound pleasant."

"Hey, M-J. Sorry, I thought it was Jim again. He knows I'm running behind, trying to get out the door. He's called three times in the last half hour."

"It's done."

"What's done?"

"The papers. They're signed and ready for the mail."

"Let me guess…You agreed to everything and are walking away with nothing."

"I don't care about his money. I don't need it. I just want to be done."

"I can't believe after all you've been through, after all he's done—"

"Anne, don't start. I refuse to dwell on the negative."

"That's what you get for marrying a man twenty years your senior. I told you when he asked you it was wrong."

"I still think he loved me, in his way."

"Think what you like. It was never meant to be. You said it yourself a hundred times: in your heart and in those damned dreams, you knew it was a mistake."

"He was good to me, for a while."

"It didn't help that he kept a constant string of mistresses."

"Enough. I'll see you in thirty minutes. And try to be more positive." She pulled her hair back and twisted it into a thick braid. Squaring her shoulders and stepping past her reflection in the patio door, she shook her head and smiled. What a life.

With one finger on the number in the phone book, she dialed O'Connell's Auto Repair. "Good morning, Mr. O'Connell. This is Marie-Justine Cantrell. Would you have time to do an oil change on my Mercedes today?" She closed the phone book and pushed it to the back corner of the desk. "Great, I'll drop it off right away. See you in a few minutes."

Systematically, she went from room to room, checking every door and window. They were locked. She pulled on a black fleece vest over her gray turtleneck, picked up the keys to her silver Mercedes, and put them in the pocket of the vest. From the center drawer of the desk, she plucked a second set of keys to leave with the car at the repair shop. She struggled with the key ring as she tried to remove her house key. The metal clasp would not release. Running late, she gave up and jammed the extra set of keys in her pocket.

Marie-Justine caressed the petals of freshly cut flowers arranged in a crystal vase on the table near the front door. "I'll be back soon and open all the windows for you."

She scanned the light pastel rooms of the small cottage. Her eyes focused on the back door. She had checked it earlier. It was locked. Still, she felt the urge to check it again.

"No. Don't do it." Refusing to allow her fears to overcome her reason, she forced herself out the front door.

For a moment, as she locked the door, her joy faded. There was a time she would have left the doors and windows open and gone her way without giving it a thought. But that time was gone. Stepping off the front porch, she said a silent prayer, hoping that those carefree days and nights might come again.

FOUR

Joe Nicoletti lit a cigarette and exhaled a cloud of smoke. It drifted across the terrace to join other clouds rising from the outdoor tables of the café on Arthur Avenue. He had tried to get a table inside, but smokers were only seated outside, forced to endure the sunshine and gentle breezes of early October. Nonsmokers were huddled inside the darkened restaurant, volunteering to be covered with the smell of home fries, onions, and bacon grease.

He leaned back, tilting his chair against a white picket fence, which rested against a gunmetal-gray bicycle rack. Four coeds at the next table chattered incessantly. As near as he could tell, each of their revelations revolved around alcohol, sex, and drugs. If their parents ever heard this nonsense, they would jerk the funding out from under them.

"More coffee?" The waitress poured before he could answer. "You're a cop, right?"

"Not anymore. Retired," Nicoletti answered without thinking. "How—"

"You were here last April with Agent Pandori. You guys sat at this same table."

Nicoletti was at a loss for words. His mouth was open, but no sound came.

"My uncle's a sergeant with the sheriff's office. I know Agent Pandori—he's a regular. Besides, he's the only FBI agent in town. Most everybody knows him." She added another splash to his cup. "So you retired from the FBI?"

"No, DEA."

"Well, let's keep that between us," she said in an exaggerated whisper. "I don't want you to scare off my customers, or half the kitchen staff, for that matter."

"You're kidding."

"Hey, this is a college town and the university is right across the street." She pointed behind him.

"Got it." He crossed his heart. "My lips are sealed. April was a long time ago. How do you remember me?"

"It was my first day working here. I spilled water all over your table. You helped me mop it up. You guys were very nice about it. Left me the biggest tip I've ever gotten. You want something to eat?"

"Not right—"

"I'll check back in a few."

He took a swig of coffee. Over the rim of the cup, he saw a bicycle closing quickly on his left. The rider was a very attractive woman—athletic, early forties—wearing a green Colorado State sweatshirt. She slammed the bike into the rack, dismounted, and nodded briskly.

"Good morning," she said without sincerity.

He tried to smile but only managed a nod, thankful she hadn't pushed the bike rack through the fence and onto his lap.

Nicoletti watched her enter the patio and toss a small backpack onto a mauve concrete table shaded by a green-and-purple umbrella. Lean and muscular, sculpted by skintight, black Lycra bicycle shorts, she strode past him, ignoring his inspection of her physique. With an air of confidence, she tossed her layered black hair, mounted the stairs to the right of his table, flung open the screen door, and entered the café.

His cell phone vibrated in his pocket. "Nicoletti."

"Hey, Nico. It's Pandori."

"No kidding."

"How was your flight from DC?"

"Delayed. I didn't get to the hotel 'til after nine. Instead of going to bed, I made the mistake of eating some lousy Chinese food. Lucky to be alive. Where are you?"

"Working. I'm gonna have to cancel. Someone found a body in the woods a few miles west of town. May be a missing person named Candice Wilson. She disappeared when you were here last April. Remember?"

"No."

"Sure you do. She was a Realtor. I got a call on it when you were over for dinner. We—"

"Yeah, I remember. Does that make you feel better?"

"Are you at the restaurant?"

"What do you think?"

"Have some home fries for me. I'll probably be tied up the rest of the morning. Can you keep yourself busy and out of trouble?"

"No problem. The scenery is just about to improve." Nicoletti looked toward the screen door and signaled the waitress for another coffee.

FIVE

A white tow truck with O'CONNELL'S AUTO REPAIR, FOREIGN AND DOMESTIC written in chipped, red paint on the side pulled up in front of the café. A woman got out of the passenger door. She was talking to the driver, but Nicoletti couldn't hear anything above the clapping of the diesel engine. She stepped onto the curb, and the truck drove off. She entered the café's patio and sat at the table under the green-and-purple umbrella.

The new arrival was dressed in jeans, a gray turtleneck, and a black fleece vest. Her chestnut hair, entwined in a loose braid, was shimmering with red highlights that vanished when she moved under the umbrella's shade.

Nicoletti stopped breathing. The woman was too familiar. Her body, her hair, the way she moved, and now the view of her face recalled to his mind the overpowering image of his wife—the center of his world, ripped from his life three years ago. So real was the image that he almost called out "Kristen."

She looked directly at him.

Had he said it out loud? He felt embarrassed, frozen, and awkward. The blood rushed to his face.

She smiled.

It's not her. Could it be?

Are you mad?

He started breathing. Combat breathing. He had been warned. If he did not stop obsessing over his wife's sudden and unexpected death, he could go mad. He had done well for the last three years, gotten his mind and emotions under control, started living and working again. He had come too far to crumble now.

He strained his eyes to see beneath the umbrella, looking carefully for discrepancies that would dispel this mirage. Finally, he relaxed. The resemblance was striking but not exact. In fact, the more he looked at the woman, the less she looked like his Kristen.

His thoughts vanished as the woman in Lycra shorts burst through the screen door carrying two coffee cups, then set them in front of the woman with the chestnut braid. They exchanged brief kisses—first one cheek, then the other—and settled into what appeared to be a cheerful and lively conversation.

Nicoletti leaned forward and tried to listen. He detected a distinct French accent in the voice of the woman with the braid.

The bike rider took a small box from her backpack and slid it across the table. Laughing and talking in a raised tone, the chestnut-haired beauty opened the box.

"Jivago," she said, pulling a tapered glass bottle of perfume from the box. "Where did you get it? Certainly not here."

"On my last trip to Denver. Between the two of us, my bottle went so fast I bought two. Now that you have your own place, it seemed silly to keep them both. Besides, today is a special occasion and I wanted to get you something."

They exchanged cheek kisses again. Nicoletti lit another cigarette to celebrate too. The women were laughing and taking turns spraying themselves with the perfume. He had no idea what the occasion was, but it smelled damn good to him.

To his right, he heard a clicking and whirring sound he recognized. It was the clicking of a camera shutter and the noise made by the drive of an automatic film advancer, two sounds he hadn't heard in years but would never forget. He spotted a young man holding an old 35mm Nikon seated across the patio. From Nicoletti's angle, it was apparent that the photographer was focusing on the women sitting under the green-and-purple umbrella. He heard the shutter snap and the film advance again.

Annoying little bastard, Nicoletti thought, as he returned his gaze to the women.

SIX

Nicoletti was startled. A man in a gray coat walked into the patio area, and as he passed the mauve table, he reached out with his right hand and touched the loose, chestnut braid, running his hand along its soft curve.

The woman did not react. Preoccupied with her animated conversation, the uninvited touch of a stranger had escaped her notice.

The man in the gray coat walked into the café without missing a step, turning his head away from Nicoletti's view. Nicoletti estimated him to be similar to his own six-foot height, maybe a little taller and a little lighter, weighing around one eighty-five or so. The man's movements were smooth—animal-like, powerful. "Predator" was the only word that came to Nicoletti's mind.

A few minutes later, the man was out of the restaurant, heading back to the street. As he passed the woman, his left hand moved toward her. She leaned toward her friend. The left hand abandoned its attempt at contact and entered the pocket of the gray coat.

Nicoletti shifted forward in his seat and pulled his legs beneath him. He was ready to pounce on the intruder. He did not know what was happening, but he knew danger. He felt the colliding of atoms all around him, setting a tingle in the air—a cosmic disturbance preceding danger that he had come to know from a lifetime of hunting criminals.

He watched the gray coat disappear into a building at the edge of the campus. The building had the name JESSE HALL prominently displayed on a sign facing the street. It was a dormitory, full of potential victims for those floating hands.

Nicoletti gave serious thought to following the man, grabbing him by the neck, and threatening him to keep his hands to himself. He could demand the gray coat's identity. *"Let me see some fucking ID, you piece of shit."* Then he would at least have a name to give to the campus police. They could put it on file for future reference should any female student report a Peeping Tom, or molester, or worse.

The urge faded as Nicoletti sipped his coffee. That's not the way police worked. If he had followed his instinct and did what he wanted to do, the police would think *he* was nuts. They'd probably cite *him* for assault on a student or unlawful detention of a citizen. After all, he wasn't a cop anymore.

He imagined the campus police's reaction. What the hell was a retired federal narcotics agent from Washington, DC, doing in Montana, roughing up law-abiding, tuition-paying students? Just because a guy touched a woman's hair, possibly by accident, and then went into a restaurant and left without buying anything, did not make him a criminal.

Not yet, Nicoletti thought.

SEVEN

Charles Durbin emerged from the rear exit of Jesse Hall. He placed the gray coat in the back of his Suburban. A thin layer of dust covered the charcoal-gray paint. He liked the way the road dust made the vehicle appear lighter in color, providing a natural camouflage.

He was excited. The meeting with Marie-Justine at the café had gone so much better than he could have ever hoped. He congratulated himself on the boldness and delicate execution of the spontaneous plan. Reaching out and touching her hair had sent a thrill through his core. The unexpected pungency of her perfume had virtually transported him into a dream. Reaching toward her a second time was greedy. He blamed the perfume for the inexcusable lapse of self-control.

He walked to the pay phone on Arthur Avenue at the entrance to the campus parking lot, no more than fifty yards from the café. He took a small pair of binoculars from his fanny pack and focused them on the two women under the green-and-purple umbrella. They were drinking coffee and laughing. He moved the binoculars from one to the other. They both excited him. But he had finally made his choice.

He dialed Marie-Justine's home number from the pay phone. The answering machine came on. Durbin listened to her sensual voice—the voice of his chosen lover.

The binoculars had been added to his ritual only recently. It brought him great excitement to hear her voice and enjoy the smooth tones of her accented English while gazing at her face so near he could kiss it.

He was so enraptured with the moment that he let the greeting end and the recording of his breathing begin. An ambulance racing down Arthur Avenue blasted its siren at a man crossing the street. Durbin slammed the receiver into its cradle. Another mistake. He looked around. No one was paying the slightest bit of attention to him.

He calmed himself with deep breathing. His hands trembled. Heat surged from under his shirt. Sweat from under his arms cooled as it slid against his rib cage.

He returned the binoculars to his pack. Too risky, he decided.

He dialed again and again, always careful to hang up before complying with her simple request to leave his name and number. He hoped that one day he would be free to leave his number so she would call him upon her return.

EIGHT

Nicoletti broke into a light jog while the ambulance raced by, his foot hitting the curb as the siren switched from wail to yelp. To his right, a pay phone receiver crashed into its cradle. He watched the flustered caller walk a few steps from the phone, only to step back and resume dialing.

Pandori's report of the discovered corpse, the siren, and the angry man at the pay phone confirmed Nicoletti's belief that all towns, no matter how tranquil they appeared on the surface, had an undercurrent of violence and anger.

Nicoletti looked back across the street at the café. He had left the patio without saying a word to the two women under the green-and-purple umbrella. Donning his best smile as he passed their table, he'd slowed his step. For some unknown reason, he had expected the woman with the chestnut braid to reach out and touch his forearm. In his mind, she calmly whispered, "*Please stay. I want to know you, again. I have so much to tell you.*" In reality, neither woman had even glanced in his direction.

"You are such a schmuck, Nicoletti," he mumbled out loud.

He consoled himself with the idea that it was a small town and he would see them again. He promised himself that the next time, he wouldn't hesitate.

"What makes you think you deserve a second chance, putz?"

To his left was the entrance to Jesse Hall and the door through which the man in the gray coat had passed. The security mechanism required an activation of the lock by some type of identity card. Nicoletti timed his approach to coincide with two coeds on their way out. They pushed open the door and he grabbed it, allowing them to exit before he entered. Did the creep belong here, or did he get in the same way?

Looking around the lobby, he realized the man could be anywhere within the dormitory. Even if someone had noticed him, everyone in the lobby was either coming in or going out; anyone who might have seen him enter the building was long gone by now.

Along the campus walkways, students moved leisurely, alone and in groups, talking and laughing. Only occasionally did one of them acknowledge Nicoletti with a nod or a brief smile.

After a few minutes of wandering aimlessly, he gave up. The guy was gone. At least Nicoletti wasn't likely to find him. The women were gone from the café patio too.

Walking across the mouth of the campus parking lot, Nicoletti had to jump back as a gray Suburban raced past him and into the street. The vehicle missed him by inches, but the driver never touched his brakes or honked his horn.

"Maybe this town is too dangerous for me," Nicoletti said.

NINE

Charles Durbin parked his gray Suburban across the street from O'Connell's Auto Repair. He scanned the building. There were no exterior security cameras. The overhead doors of the garage were opened wide. Inside, two vehicles were suspended on lifts, hanging like carcasses in the dark. O'Connell, working alone, moved from the undercarriage of one car to the other, singing loudly and swaying to the country music that blared from the shop radio.

Marie-Justine's silver Mercedes was parked in a fenced area to the right of the garage. Seven or eight other cars were parked closer to the open doors. How much time did he have? Was it worth the risk? He put the Suburban in reverse but kept his foot on the brake. This was his chance. He had to risk it. Waiting for O'Connell to focus his efforts on one of the cars, he let his mind wander.

Months earlier, when Marie-Justine moved into her home, he already had a key. But she had unexpectedly changed the locks, and for over a month, he had been denied access to her yellow-and-white cottage.

When he first realized that she was looking for a new place to live, he had been upset. He followed her for several weeks as she shopped for a house. He had tried to silently will her to remain living in Anne Bertone's home. He liked the convenience of having both women simultaneously at his disposal. He enjoyed watching them at night, walking from room to room, separated from him by only the sheer screens of open windows and darkness.

He also liked standing in the heavily treed lot behind Anne's house during the day, watching them lay side by side on Anne's back deck in the hot July sun. He would crouch in the shade behind the foliage while they talked and laughed, smearing sunscreen on each other. Sometimes he could smell the scent of coconut from the lotion.

But daylight was more dangerous for him. He had to be conscious of both of them, each just an accidental glance away from seeing him. It was quite stimulating—exciting, actually—but too risky.

He had finally decided he would be better off if they lived apart. He would have two locations for pleasure. From then on, he was in a better mood as he watched the house-buying excursions.

On several occasions, they had returned to the same yellow-and-white cottage, sometimes with a Realtor, sometimes without. In the front yard was a blue-and-white sign:

FOR SALE BY FITZGERALD REALTY / CALL JENNY

Then one Sunday, the Fitzgerald Realty sign was obscured by a banner that read UNDER CONTRACT. The black Realtor's lockbox on the front door was still in place. Marie-Justine and Anne walked in and out of the house, raked the yard, and chatted with the elderly woman living next door, as if they had already taken up residence.

Durbin had checked the Sunday paper for the Fitzgerald Realty ads. Along with the property listings, the company was kind enough to provide him with the name and a photograph of each of the Realtors in the local office. He quickly found the photo of Jenny. Jenny Garland.

He knew her. She was a bit overweight—zaftig, one might say—in her early forties, and had bleached blond hair in need of moisturizing and a good cut. She was married to the local police chief but not very happily, according to the confidences she shared while sipping tea in Durbin's kitchen as he groomed her Yorkshire terrier.

At first, Jenny was skeptical about his sudden interest in buying another house.

"As an investment," he had said to quell her curiosity.

As they eventually began to visit properties for sale she would occasionally ask about his past. Deftly he would change the subject to her personal life, a subject on which he knew she could ramble for hours.

He only requested to see properties that were listed by Fitzgerald Realty, and in particular, the ones that Jenny had listed herself. This way, he was almost guaranteed that the lockboxes on each front door would be opened by the same combination. He stood as close as he dared. She opened one front door after another, and each time, he picked up a new number. After the fifth house, he had the combination he needed.

He had driven to the yellow-and-white cottage. There was only one lock on the door: a dead bolt. The lock box yielded the key on the first try. Twenty minutes later, he had returned the key to the box and tried the newly cut duplicate. It hung up at first, but after a few twists, it turned the tumblers of the dead bolt smoothly.

Marie-Justine moved into the cottage the first week in August. From then until early September, Durbin was able to wander through her house and touch her things at will, provided he was cautious not to be seen. He had been tempted to enter at night while she slept. He would have, except that he did not like the idea of a confrontation should she awake and find him hovering. Until recently, he had not been ready for that. Instead, he allowed his hunger to grow slowly. He only explored while she was out, being careful not to become too lost in his musings and always leaving well before her return.

Three weeks ago, he followed her to an evening concert on campus. Once he was sure she was inside the music building, he headed directly to the cottage. Delighted he would have several hours alone, he hummed as he approached her door. But he couldn't get in. He tried twice before he realized the dead bolt had been changed and a new doorknob presented a second lock.

At first he had been frightened. Why had she changed the lock? Had he been seen? Did she notice something out of place? Maybe the old lady next door had seen him. He dismissed his fears. He was too careful, too skilled. He should have anticipated the locks would be changed. He had been lucky to get the time he had enjoyed. In other cities, the locks would have been replaced before the new owner moved in.

Now, as he entered O'Connell's Auto Repair, he was close to possessing all he needed to resume his foraging. Behind the wooden counter were two pegboards—

one marked DROP OFF, the other PICK UP. He lifted the Mercedes ring from the drop-off board and placed it in his pocket. He turned to leave.

"Can I help you?" O'Connell's voice held a hint of suspicion.

"Need an oil change. Got time today?" Durbin tried not to look the mechanic in the eye.

"Sorry, not today. Can ya come back Monday?" O'Connell said, wiping his hands on a greasy towel.

"Monday is good." Durbin stepped out the open doorway. "Might stop by again later and see if you can work me in."

"No sense in that. I'll be lucky to finish the ones I've got stacked in the yard before five tonight."

Thirty minutes later, Durbin replaced the Mercedes keys on the drop-off board. O'Connell never noticed.

TEN

Nicoletti wandered the residential area bordering the campus and studied the local architecture. He made mental notes of features that he hoped to one day include in his own peaceful retreat. In the six months since his retirement, it had become his habit to imagine building a home in which he could enjoy his remaining years. It had begun to take shape first in his mind, systematically incorporating and abandoning various design ideas, and then on paper.

He drew floor plans and elevations whenever time allowed. He had plenty of time. In his new life as an investigator for a law firm in Washington, DC, he seemed to have more time on his hands than was good for him. In the last few weeks, he had been concentrating on gardens and outdoor patio areas: teak benches and tables, stone walls and archways, slate and brick. It all intrigued him. These were the things he looked for in the side and rear yards near the university as he patiently walked the streets of the quiet neighborhood.

After two hours of walking every street and alley he could find, Nicoletti began to tire. His pace and powers of observation slowed. Distracted by a trellis covered with roses, a piece of uneven concrete in the sidewalk caught and held the toe of his right foot, and he was propelled headlong into a thick hedge of hemlock.

Pulling himself from the evergreen branches, he heard Vivaldi. The music flowed from the open doors and windows of a small, pale yellow cottage with white trim, partially concealed from the street by the hemlock hedge. The cottage was set amid the autumn remains of what had been a lush garden. The flower beds were divided by a brick walk leading to the front porch and side patio.

Through the hemlock boughs he saw a woman sitting on the patio in the sun. To the right of her chair was a metal table with a stone top. Nicoletti recognized her as the woman with the chestnut braid from the café.

She was dressed in white shorts and a pink tank top. Her tan legs held Nicoletti's attention until she extended a taut dancer's arm gracefully to her right to pick up a teacup from the table. As she brought it to her lips, he cast an admiring glance along her toned body, her muscles long and smooth.

He felt a light tapping on his left shoulder and sprung back from the hedge, landing in a defensive position, his body angled toward the imagined attacker, his hands raised to protect his head and chest.

Confronting him was an elderly woman no more than five feet tall. Her body was positioned in an exaggerated offensive stance, her left foot forward. A red-and-white checked apron clung loosely to her thin build. She waved a broomstick dangerously close to the tip of his nose.

"Are you looking for something, young man?" she asked, holding the broom across her body, ready to parry any advance he might attempt.

"No, I just tripped on the sidewalk and sort of stumbled up against this hedge here." He gestured as if to emphasize the innocence of his behavior with the use of sign language. He heard the phone ring behind the hedge and saw a blur of white, pink, and tan head into the house from the patio.

"I've told the city several times about the condition of the walk. A person could break their neck just going to the store."

"There's no doubt about that. Sorry if I gave you a start." He delivered the sentence in his best country boy twang and began to retreat toward the street.

"Where you from, mister? New York?" She advanced on his position.

"I was born there, but I'm from a little bit of all over." He refused to drop the unsuccessful twang.

"What brings you to Missoula?" She was relentless.

"Came to look at the university. Might take a teaching position here next semester." Well, he might, he thought, if he knew anything worth teaching and if someone offered him a job.

"You don't look like a professor to me." She started to point the boom handle in his direction. "How old are you?"

"Fifty."

"I wouldn't have guessed that old."

"Thanks," he said, hoping she meant it as a compliment.

"Well, if you do end up here, come on back and visit me. My name's Jaeger." She leaned toward him and spoke softly for the first time. "I might even invite my neighbor to join us." She pointed the broomstick in the direction of the yellow and white cottage and smiled at Nicoletti. "She's a professor over there too. A scientist... real smart...a real lady, sweet and kind as they come." She poked the stick at his shoulder. "That'll give you a chance to talk to her instead of just lookin' at her."

"Sounds like a date. I'll look forward to it. Take care." Nicoletti eased back slowly, though he would have preferred to run away. He decided Jaeger was an alias and the old woman must be retired KGB, relocated to Montana after the fall of the Berlin Wall. He checked the tips of her shoes for poison-dipped daggers.

Through the hedge he saw the patio was vacant. Mrs. Jaeger was still talking, but Nicoletti stopped listening. Now all he had to do was figure out how to get back to his hotel.

ELEVEN

Marie-Justine continued talking on the phone as she looked out the patio door, straining to see through the hedge. She was curious whom Mrs. Jaeger was accosting.

"Did you check with Jim? Are we on for tomorrow night?" Marie-Justine said, tugging at the legs of her white shorts.

"I'm sorry, M-J. He's committed us to a dinner at the Bedford's. Jim swears he told me about it the other night. I must have forgotten. I've been so preoccupied with the book; I guess it just slipped by me."

"Another dinner at Dean Bedford's house? Won't tonight with the academic crowd at Dean Hawkins' party be enough for him?"

"Tonight is the sociology department, and it's just cocktails. Tomorrow is literature and a more intimate dinner for twenty. I don't know how much more I can take."

"Well, don't worry. It's okay." She hid her disappointment. "I guess I can't compete with Jim's need to kneel at the feet of the dean of the literature department." Marie-Justine never tried to hide her opinion of Anne's choice of companions, and her opinion of Jim Reynolds was especially critical.

"I know you're disappointed. Maybe we could do something next week to celebrate."

"Sounds good. We can toast to my divorce tonight at the Hawkins' party. Tomorrow I will celebrate alone. Tomorrow it will be 'champagne for one' at Chez Margot."

"You'll be drinking French champagne while I'm sipping a thick and overly sweet California cabernet with the dullest people in town? Don't rub it in."

"Anne, you're not going to believe this. Remember the man at the café this morning?" She focused on the scene on the other side of the hedge. "The guy with the salt-and-pepper hair, sitting at the corner table?"

"Do I remember? Broad shoulders, soft brown eyes...I'm just distracted, honey, not dead."

"I think my neighbor, Mrs. Jaeger, is out on the sidewalk, hitting him with a broom."

"She's probably trying to drive him into her house. Tell her to leave him alone. He's mine. I saw him first."

"But you have Jim."

"I'll work a trade-in," Anne said. "Don't let Mrs. Jaeger beat us to the punch. Shall we pick you up about 7:45?"

"I'm going with Dr. Kimba. Remember? I agreed to be his escort for the evening."

"Of course I remember." Her voice said she didn't. "Hey, do you need a ride to go get your car?"

"No, Mr. O'Connell said he would drop it off on his way home."

"Okay. Now go out and save that hunk from your neighbor's clutches. Invite him to the party tonight. Wouldn't he be a pleasant change? And don't give me that 'I feel like I know him' nonsense."

"I *do* know him from somewhere."

"I didn't believe it this morning and I still don't buy it now. See you tonight, about eight. And don't use too much of that perfume." Anne hung up.

Marie-Justine stepped back onto the patio. The commotion in Mrs. Jaeger's driveway was over and the combatants were gone.

If Anne was too tied up with Jim to celebrate with her, so be it. She was not going to be sad. She had been waiting years for this day. Her lawyer had called from Los Angeles yesterday with the news that she and Dr. David Cantrell were officially divorced. The paperwork that she signed this morning was a mere formality. A celebration was in order and she was going to have one tomorrow night, with or without her best and oldest friend.

She called the Chez Margot Restaurant and made a reservation for the following evening at seven. She filled a wine glass halfway with the pale yellow crispness of cold Mâcon-Villages. She looked again for the stranger she thought she knew. Accepting that he was gone, she sat down to read in the warm afternoon sun.

.   .   .

A dusty, gray Suburban pulled away from the curb and rolled slowly down the tree-lined street. Charles Durbin followed the gray-haired man he had seen peeking through the hemlock hedge. When it was obvious the man was heading toward downtown, Durbin abandoned the chase in favor of returning to see the object of his desire.

Slinking down behind the wheel as he drove past the yellow-and-white cottage, Durbin smiled as he saw Marie-Justine sitting on her patio in the afternoon sun. He checked his watch. He was out of time. He had an appointment at four on the other side of town. A terrier with bad teeth and gums needed a scaling.

"I will be back tonight, my dear," he whispered as he drove away.

TWELVE

Wet from the shower, a towel wrapped around his waist, Nicoletti answered his hotel room phone.

"Hey, Nico, it's Lenny." The upbeat voice of Lenny Pandori brought a smile to Nicoletti's face. "Where the hell have you been? I've been trying to reach you all afternoon."

"Just walking around town." Pressing the phone between his shoulder and his ear, he tugged at the towel to stretch it around his waist. Either hotels were skimping on the size of their bath towels or he was eating too much pasta.

"Great little town, don't you think? Nice place to settle down," Pandori said.

"Yeah, very nice." The towel sprung loose and fell to the floor. Nicoletti shook it, then wrapped it around again, this time holding it closed with one hand.

"Don't forget the reception tonight. Want me to pick you up?"

"No. I'll find my way there. How's Liz?" Nicoletti abandoned his struggle with the postage stamp-sized towel and pulled on a pair of sweat pants and a T-shirt, trying to keep his ear to the receiver.

"She's fine. Out of town until next week, visiting her sister in Billings. So I'm a bachelor once again. Make sure you're at the Hawkins' house at 7:30 sharp. The rest of the guests won't show till eight. That'll give you a chance to talk to the dean one-on-one. He's really looking forward to seeing you again."

"I'll bet."

"Don't be so fucking negative. See you later."

Nicoletti dried the phone, opened the drapes, and turned on the desk lamp. From his briefcase he took a small, dark green velvet pouch. He untied the drawstring and emptied the contents of the pouch into his left hand.

He sat on the edge of the bed and stared at the small, gold wedding band and delicate wooden rosary in his hand. He raised the gold ring to his lips and kissed it. Then, taking the rosary in his right hand, he began a ritual he had practiced since Kristen's death. A ritual that signaled an attempt to connect, like dialing the phone and hoping she would answer.

His fingers moved from one bead to the next until he clasped the rosary and gold ring with both hands. He spoke to an empty room.

"Kristen, I'm in Missoula again. I guess you know that. I'm still thinking of taking the teaching job here. Actually, I'm not thinking of it; I have pretty much made up my mind. If the offer is good I'll do it. Lenny thinks he's helping me get a new start. Do I need a new start?

"I talked to the kids last night. They're all fine. Kristy is thinking of quitting her job and opening up a pastry shop. I don't know what to tell her other than 'Do what will make you happy.' You better give her a little nudge, if you can. The boys are the same as usual, so I guess all is well here."

He stood up and shifted the rosary into his left hand with the gold ring. He started to walk around the room, then returned to the edge of the bed and sat down again.

"I saw a woman today. She reminded me of you. Not just the way she looked. It was more the way I felt when I looked at her. I know after all this time it's a little crazy, and maybe it is...maybe not. For some reason I don't think it is. Anyway, I just thought I'd mention it. Okay?

"I've got to get ready to go to some cocktail party with Lenny. I won't drink too much so don't worry." He put his wife's ring and rosary back in the pouch, pulled the strings tight, and placed it next to his cell phone in the briefcase.

THIRTEEN

Dean Hawkins and his wife lived in a large Tudor-style house. English landscapes hung on heavily plastered walls. The dark parquet floors were covered with Oriental rugs beneath uncomfortable-looking antique furniture.

Guests moved in slow waves from the living room into the study, then through what the dean's too-thin wife called "the sunroom," a glassed conservatory filled with flowering plants, small trees, and wicker furniture. The rooms on the main floor opened onto a wraparound deck. The rapidly cooling night air pushed into the house from all sides.

Nicoletti watched the guests. To him they seemed like floating icebergs, breaking free from one cluster of friends and acquaintances only to temporarily attach themselves to another. At each stop the floaters would shake hands or nod, then engage in the conversation, sip drinks, and munch on crackers topped with various creamed spreads. Small trays of food and wine were passed from cluster to cluster by students dressed as bistro waiters, in black and white.

Lenny Pandori was responsible for Nicoletti being invited to Missoula as a guest lecturer for the Western States Law Enforcement Conference, hosted by the university. He was also responsible for leaving Nicoletti alone with Dean Hawkins. From seven thirty to eight, the dean updated Nicoletti on the progress of his plans to develop an integrated criminology degree within the department of sociology. Last spring, Pandori had convinced the dean that Nicoletti was just the right combination of practical experience and academic degrees to be recruited into the new program as an adjunct professor. Pandori was now on a mission to convince Nicoletti.

What Nicoletti had imagined would be a brief conversation with Hawkins had turned into an eternity. He applied all his powers of concentration to follow the dean's dissertation, but all he really wanted to do was eat. He tried several of the hors d'oeuvres, unable to tell what type of paste they carried.

Whenever the dean was distracted, acknowledging new arrivals, Nicoletti eagerly helped himself to a canapé from every tray within reach until he grabbed one that his senses were definitely able to identify as rotten salmon mixed with cream cheese and dill. He had gotten it halfway into his mouth when his nose warned him to throw it on the floor and kill it.

Unfortunately, at that moment, Dean Hawkins returned to his side to expound upon the benefits of living in Missoula. Nicoletti could feel his gag reflex beginning to kick in. His eyes started to water. He needed to get the fish paste off his tongue as soon as possible. His survival instincts ordered him to spit it against the dean's tweed jacket. He swallowed without chewing and guzzled half a glass of red wine in hopes of killing the toxins. Hawkins kept talking, oblivious to Nicoletti's brush with death.

By 8:45 he had already had too much to drink. Hours of walking, two cups of coffee, no breakfast, no lunch, no dinner, a glass of water, followed by half a bottle of Bordeaux in his hotel room had set the stage. Several more glasses while listening to the dean had started to tip the scales. The absorption power of the finger food was no match for the wine. He wanted to head for the kitchen to find some bread and drink a glass of water. The taste of the salmon paste lingered. Maybe he could wipe his mouth out with a paper towel.

Dean Hawkins finally moved on to his other guests giving Nicoletti a moment to objectively assess the attendees. It was the type of gathering he was usually careful to avoid. People he did not know, living in a universe divorced from his own. A room full of strangers he was destined to alienate if he tried to be sociable. Normally, by now he would have grabbed his coat and made a quick exit. But tonight he was stuck. Pandori expected him to be there and to participate as an adult.

He had hardly a moment to himself before a woman replaced the dean at his side.

"Hi. I'm Jenny Garland. You must be Pandori's friend Nico." She took his hand and gave it a hard shake. "That's my husband over there, Peter Garland; he's the chief of police."

Stacked heels and teased hair made Police Chief Peter Garland's wife just tall enough to send her perfume and bleached blond wisps into Nicoletti's nostrils. He tried not to sneeze as he extricated his hand from her grasp and mumbled something he hoped would pass for a cordial greeting.

She leaned toward him, swinging a glass of chardonnay. "Most of them are assholes." Jenny Garland breathed against his chest as she motioned the stemmed glass across the panorama of guests. She then proceeded to provide the least flattering, ribald commentary she could muster about every one of them. "Not that they're all so bad... Just trying to fill you in." She grabbed a passing waiter and swapped her empty glass for a full one.

Nicoletti smiled and looked straight ahead. His peripheral vision was sufficient to keep her ample cleavage in view. He dared not look down. From across the room, Chief Garland was looking directly at him. He felt the stare to be a little hostile and knew it would only get worse if he were caught gawking at the tanned flesh that was spilling over the scooped neckline of Garland's wife's dress.

"They think all us locals are beneath them." She stood up straight and pulled her shoulders back.

Nicoletti gave in; he had to look. He could feel the chief bristle, but it was worth it.

"You think I'm fat?" she asked.

"I think you look terrific."

"Mr. Perfect over there thinks I'm fat."

She looked at her husband, who moved to the far side of the room and started talking to a woman with short dark hair. Nicoletti recognized her as the bike rider from the café.

"I see he's finally located Princess Anne. That's what I call her. Anne Bertone is her name. I wonder where Little Swiss Miss is tonight."

"Miss who?" Nicoletti asked.

"Annie's friend Marie-Justine. I call her Little Swiss Miss, you know, like the hot chocolate. She's from Switzerland. You can't miss her. She's like a fashion model with a PhD in her back pocket. She and Annie are usually inseparable."

"You know them?" Nicoletti asked. After twenty minutes of providing the most intimate details on everyone in the room, Jenny had finally hit on a topic of real interest to Nicoletti.

"Sure do, darling. Like I told you, I know everybody. Annie and I grew up together. You wouldn't know it to talk to her, but she's a local. Well, at least till she went away to college. She dated my husband in high school. Once they broke up, Pete and I started going out, and as they say, the rest is history."

"So Annie lives here now?"

"Sort of. She moved back last spring after her mother died. She really lives in Denver. Has a big job with *The Denver Post*, but she's on a year's sabbatical to finish writing some book on the history of her family."

"And her friend?" Nicoletti pushed for as much information as possible.

"Swiss Miss is a friend of hers from grad school. She's in the middle of a divorce from some big-shot surgeon in LA. She just moved here last summer."

"You don't like them?"

"Oh, I love Annie. We were the best of pals in high school. And Marie-Justine couldn't be sweeter. But the two of them are so damn gorgeous, a real woman has a tough time competing." She poked Nicoletti's rib cage. "Know what I mean?"

"I don't think you'd have a tough time competing with anyone." He clinked the side of his wine glass against hers. Nicoletti couldn't help but grin. He liked Jenny. She was disarmingly direct and funny. He noticed Peter Garland was looking at him again. He tried to will the grin off his face, but it had a mind of its own.

FOURTEEN

The chief and Anne Bertone were heading directly toward them. Garland was about six foot four and probably weighed in somewhere near two fifty. He carried a rocks glass half full of scotch that all but disappeared in his oversized left hand. Anne, who was probably five foot seven, looked tiny walking next to him. Her muscular legs pulled tight against her dark blue skirt. Her upper body was held firmly inside a fitted, white cotton blouse. Nicoletti noted her trim waist accentuated her full breasts.

Jenny's elbow again found Nicoletti's rib cage. "Snap out of it Romeo. You're drooling."

"It must be the water," he mumbled.

"Honey, this is Joe Nicoletti. Nico, this is my husband, Pete, and my friend Annie." Jenny reached out and seductively touched the chief on his left bicep.

The woman pushed her short dark hair from her face with her left hand and extended her right to provide a firm handshake. "Anne Bertone. A pleasure to meet you, Mr. Nicoletti. I've heard a lot about you from Len Pandori. You're the famous detective he's trying to bring to the university."

"I don't know how famous I am, but remind me to thank Lenny just before I strangle him."

"Annie, where is your boyfriend?" Jenny said, obviously intending to break the spell Anne was casting over Nicoletti.

"Jim is here somewhere. I lost track of him while I was talking to your husband," Anne shot back. "And he's not my boyfriend; he's just a friend," she said directly to Nicoletti.

"So you're Lenny Pandori's buddy," Chief Garland said. He clamped down on Nicoletti's hand just hard enough to convey a warning that the chief considered these two women to be under his protection from carpetbaggers. "I'm sorry I missed you on your last visit."

Nicoletti managed a smile as he pried loose his hand.

"Had to cancel our breakfast meeting," Garland said. "That was the morning Candice Wilson was reported missing." He lowered his voice. "We may have discovered her body, or what's left of it, this morning."

"Lenny mentioned that earlier. Any new leads?"

"I heard how you saved his life a few years back." Garland ignored the question.

"You saved Lenny's life?" Jenny leaned in Nicoletti's direction.

"It was a long time ago." Nicoletti tried to back up but was halted by the fireplace mantel jabbing into his shoulder blade. He grasped his wine glass more firmly, feeling a little more intoxicated than he had before. He noted that Garland looked a little glassy-eyed; maybe the chief had also had too much to drink.

"The way I heard it, Lenny was shot in the leg by a drug dealer during a raid." He turned from one woman to the other as he reenacted what he imagined had been the scenario. "The shooter was standing over Lenny, who was lying on the floor. The dealer was pointing a shotgun at Lenny's chest, just about to finish him off, when Joe came in the room and shot the son of a bitch in the head."

"You killed him?" Jenny pushed her chest in Nicoletti's direction.

"Stone dead." Chief Garland shook Nicoletti's hand again, this time more gently. "Shot him in the eye and blew out the back of the bastard's head." Garland was now grinning and nodding at Nicoletti.

Nicoletti looked Garland in the eye but did not respond. He avoided looking at Anne or Jenny. He never cared for men who boasted about violence, especially if their information was secondhand. He was at a loss as to how to comment with any measure of civility.

Lenny Pandori stepped between Nicoletti's stare and the chief's inebriated grin. "Hey, guys, sorry to interrupt." Pandori was holding two glasses of wine in his left hand and leaning heavily on the cane that extended from his right. "Nico, there is someone I want you to meet." He handed Anne one of the wine glasses and gave the other to Jenny. "Excuse us, folks. Anne, Jenny, you ladies look lovely this evening." He pulled on Nicoletti. "I just need to borrow my buddy for a minute."

He ushered Nicoletti through the study and out onto the deck. The moonlight washed across them with the brightness of mid-afternoon.

"Thanks," Nicoletti said.

"The least I could do."

"Chief Garland is an ass." Nicoletti breathed deeply, regaining his composure.

"He's all right once you get to know him. How'd you like his wife, Jenny? Is she a kick in the ass or what?" Pandori said, lightening the mood.

"She's a riot. In less than a half hour, she gave me the rundown on all the communists, socialists, libertarians, adulterers, and gays in the room. And those tits…"

"Oh, you noticed?" Pandori laughed. "She's definitely a wealth of community knowledge. And she's a Realtor. Knows every property on the market within fifty miles. So when you're ready to invest in a house…"

"Don't push it, buddy. I'm getting the message. Although, I'll tell you, I wouldn't mind doing a little house hunting in Anne Bertone's neighborhood."

"There'll be plenty of time to visit with Anne later. But there really are a few other people I'd like you to meet. Wait here." Pandori walked back toward the house.

Nicoletti watched his friend struggle to maneuver his legs over the threshold and Oriental carpets. Pandori's condition had deteriorated considerably since they had last been together.

Nicoletti leaned on the sturdy railing of the dean's redwood deck. The night air cleared his head just enough for him to realize his nose and upper lip were numb. He thought about dumping his wine glass onto the evergreen shrubbery. He looked across the lawn toward the tree line at the edge of the property. The moonlight was so bright that it turned the landscape into sharp-edged geometric blocks of silver and black.

"Nico, you remember our resident psychiatrist, Dr. Jason Kimba," Pandori said.

Nicoletti turned to greet a thin, elderly man with a gray walrus moustache and a head of wild white hair. Standing next to the dark and stocky Pandori, they reminded Nicoletti of a pair of salt and pepper shakers he had once seen in a gift shop next to a basket of rubber alligators.

"Dr. Kimba." Nicoletti extended his hand. "Good to see you again."

"Mr. Nicoletti. Or is it Dr. Nicoletti?"

"Nico is what I answer to."

"I always ask," Kimba said. "The room behind us is so full of pompous asses who insist on being called 'doctor' that I've considered abandoning the title in order to preserve it." The elderly man shook with a frail hand.

"Doc here is the only one in the place who actually went to medical school," Pandori said. "You remember, Nico, I sent you his article on the sentencing phase of serial killer trials."

Nicoletti did remember. He also remembered the email reply he had sent Pandori, critiquing the article.

"I greatly appreciated your comments," Kimba said. "It's not often an academic gets a chance to receive feedback from someone in the field—from someone who has actually investigated serial murders." Kimba rested his back on the railing. "As I recall, you started your critique with the rather terse phrase, 'This is the kind of bullshit that keeps these psychos from getting the chair!' Is that about right?"

Nicoletti looked at Pandori. "Can't you keep anything to yourself?"

"No, dear sir," Dr. Kimba said. "Quite well-spoken and to the point." He clapped his hand atop Nicoletti's and patted it.

"I'll be right back." Pandori walked into the house.

For a few minutes, Nicoletti attempted to qualify his criticism of the article, explaining that although he tried to appreciate the necessity of presenting a serial killer's distorted childhood to the court as mitigation during the sentencing phase of the trial, he could not.

"It's quite all right," Kimba interrupted. "I've given the entire matter a great deal of thought since the article was published, and I am recently leaning toward adopting your position."

"Why?" Nicoletti asked.

"Some new information has presented itself and has caused me to rethink the entire matter. I am beginning to believe that the evil manifested in these creatures should be promptly and permanently eliminated. Maybe it should be studied briefly for academic purposes but not excused or allowed to—"

"Dr. Kimba," a delicately accented voice interrupted. "Len Pandori asked if you would join him in the conservatory. He has something he wishes to discuss with you."

The woman stepped onto the deck. Her chestnut hair was pulled tight against her head and looked wet in the moonlight. Her high cheekbones and dark eyes stirred a memory inside Nicoletti. She was wearing a black blouse with a mandarin collar and tailored, black slacks with high-heeled shoes. Her full lips looked moist and firm. "Stunning" was the word that came to Nicoletti.

"Ah, my dear, let me introduce you to—"

"Joseph Nicoletti," she said as she reached for his extended hand. "Justine Junot."

"Justine, a pleasure to meet you."

She took his hand in such a way that he realized after a moment they were not shaking hands; they were holding hands.

"Well, since you two seem to know each other, I will try to be of use to someone else. Mr. Nicoletti, I would very much like to continue our conversation, a little later perhaps. There is something quite important I need to discuss with you." He turned and entered the house without waiting for a reply.

Marie-Justine released Nicoletti's hand. "Come with me to the kitchen. I think we could both use a bite to eat." She took the half-full wine glass from his hand. "What shall I fix for you?"

Chief Garland caught up with them as they entered the kitchen. He did not appear to have sobered up and his voice was harsh, the words whispered. "You know, Nicoletti, I was thinking… you showed up in April just when Candice Wilson disappeared. Not a trace of her for months. Now you're back in town and, like magic, her body is discovered."

"What's your point?"

"Nothing. Just an interesting coincidence."

"To tell you the truth, Chief, I don't believe in coincidence."

"Neither do I, Nicoletti. Neither do I."

FIFTEEN

Charles Durbin drove past the yellow-and-white cottage three times before parking two blocks away. He walked at a steady, unhurried pace beneath the overhanging trees, stepping from shadow to shadow, avoiding unnecessary exposure, finally stopping at the hemlock hedge. He scanned the street and adjacent houses, looking for the observant eyes of nosy neighbors. The night was still. The houses were quiet.

He moved quickly along the brick path, from the hedge to the porch. Using a gloved hand, he loosened the bulb of the overhead light. The front door plunged into darkness. The stark light of the moon cut across the edge of the porch. He stood motionless, listening and watching. He pulled the newly cut keys from his pocket. In a moment, he was inside.

He shut off the desk lamp and the light in the kitchen. Now, except for the moonlight filtering through the sheer curtains, the cottage was in darkness. He returned to the front door and removed his leather gloves.

"Marie-Justine, I'm home," he called into the dark. He extended his arms, opening them wide, then closed them in a circle and pulled them toward his chest. He wrapped his empty arms around his waist and shoulder. "I missed you too," he whispered. He pulled his right hand from his shoulder and rubbed it lightly against his left cheek. He closed the hand, brought it to his lips, and kissed it tenderly at first, then with greater force.

"Show me what you have been doing while I was away." He eased his head back from his hand. Extending his left arm, he moved in the half light toward the kitchen as if being pulled by an invisible force.

He stood next to the empty kitchen table and pretended to lift an object in his left hand. He examined it then turned toward the sink. "Darling, you shouldn't have. It's so extravagant." He set the imaginary object on the table and embraced himself again.

From the refrigerator, he took an open bottle of white wine. "To love," he said as he drank from the bottle. He took a dish towel from the counter and wiped the bottle, returned it to the refrigerator, then wiped the door handle. He folded the towel and placed it back on the counter. Bored with the kitchen, he walked into the bedroom.

At the foot of the bed, Marie-Justine's folded nightgown lay atop a wooden chest. Durbin lifted the delicate garment with both hands and raised it to his face. Slowly, he pulled it closer as he inhaled deeply. The scent of sleep mixed with her perfume urged him once again into his fantasy. He set the garment on the chest and opened the closet.

He chose a dress he had always favored—sheer, but not too revealing. It was a sleeveless, lavender summer frock that had allowed him to glimpse the side of her bare breast one summer afternoon as he spied on her in the bookstore on Fifth Street. He held the dress against his chest, gradually lifting it toward his face, breathing in her perfume, musky with the memory of summer.

He began to dance, twirling slowly as he held the gauze-like layers hard against his body. He bent forward, allowing the fabric to drape across his left forearm. He buried his face into the bosom of the dress and hummed softly. He turned the front of the dress away from his body and took hold of a tiny turquoise star that was attached to the zipper. He held the dress up with his left hand, and with his right, he tugged gently on the turquoise star until the zipper was completely down to the small of the back. He felt a growing heat in his loins and dropped the dress to the floor.

The bathroom was too dark. He turned on a tiny nightlight attached to an outlet on the wall near the tile floor. He sat on the edge of the tub and pulled the wicker laundry hamper between his legs. Slowly, he opened the hamper and peered inside: a damp, green bath towel, a gray turtleneck, a pair of white shorts, and a pink shirt. One by one he lifted the items into the amber light and caressed them as he robbed them of their perfume with his heavy breath before dropping them at his feet.

His heart quickened. He felt the blood rush to his face as he lifted a flesh-colored bra from the hamper. He imagined it still held the shape of her breasts as he pushed it toward his face. He caressed the silken fabric with his lips and kissed the front of each cup. He unbuttoned his shirt and held the bra against his chest. With the smooth, sheer fabric in each hand, he moved it lightly across his skin. His nipples hardened and he began to massage his own breasts.

His left hand plunged into the hamper and grabbed a pair of pale blue silk panties. He brought them hungrily to his mouth. He closed his eyes and breathed in the perfume, searching frantically for her scent. His tongue probed the smooth fabric, and the wetness of his mouth moistened the silk.

He slid off the tub and kneeled on the hard tile. Spinning on his knees, he scattered the discarded clothing across the floor. His forearms crashed against the edge of the tub as he held the bra against his face. With his right hand, he forced the blue panties into his trousers and wrapped himself in their damp silkiness. He spread his knees and hunched his back as he thrust against the side of the tub. The smoothness of the fabric let his hand glide across his skin. The sound of blood rushing and throbbing in his head drowned out reality. He and Marie-Justine were two souls lost in their passion, one in his love.

SIXTEEN

"And...?" Marie-Justine said. "Dr. Kimba?" She touched his shoulder.

"What? I'm sorry, my dear. What were we talking about?"

"You were listing the reasons why the university board should approve Dean Hawkins' proposal to establish a criminology degree within his department. Then you started to say something about the role of psychology, and you just stopped midsentence and slowed the car to a crawl."

"I must call Mr. Nicoletti in the morning." He pulled the Volvo to the curb in front of the yellow-and-white cottage and turned off the engine.

"You said that earlier, and I told you I am taking him on a hike early tomorrow."

"Yes, of course you did. When do you think you will be back?"

"Early afternoon. We could stop at your house on our way back to his hotel."

"No." His voice was forceful. Then softer, with more control, he continued, "No. I will leave a message for him, and he can call me whenever you get back. If not, I will speak to him after his lecture Monday morning." He smiled, trying to remove any hint of urgency in his voice. "Didn't you turn on the porch light when we left?"

"It must have burned out."

"I'll walk you in."

"That's not necessary—"

"I insist, my dear." He tried to keep his voice as calm and natural as he could. He waited a moment after Marie-Justine closed the car door and the dome light went out. He reached into the glove compartment, removed a two-shot derringer, and slid it into his jacket pocket.

Once inside, Marie-Justine tried to relax her muscles that had tensed as she approached the darkened porch of the house. Everything appeared to be as she had left it.

"Would you like something to drink? Maybe some coffee?" She took the scarf from her neck and laid it on the back of the desk chair.

Dr. Kimba did not answer. He walked ahead of her into the kitchen, keeping his right hand in his jacket pocket. "May I use your bathroom?"

"Of course, but you'll have to excuse any mess you find." She turned on the kitchen faucet and filled a glass with water. "Would you like something to drink?"

Again he did not answer. She walked into the bedroom and turned on the light. She took a long sip of the cool water, then placed the glass on the nightstand. The folding door to her closet was partially opened. She reached out to close it but quickly withdrew her arm as if recoiling from the sudden snarl of an animal once thought to be harmless. She felt someone standing behind her. She froze, afraid to turn and look.

"No, nothing for me, my dear. I think I have consumed all the liquid refreshment I can stand for one evening," Dr. Kimba said from the doorway. "Are you all right? You look pale."

"I'm fine. I just don't like coming home in the dark."

"Well, there are few of us who do. It is perfectly natural. When you get to a point where you are afraid to go out of your house, call me for an appointment." He chuckled.

"Would you think me silly if I asked you to stay for a moment while I look around a bit?" She kept her eye on the closet door.

"I'll stand right here. It has been a long time since I've been called upon to protect a damsel in distress." He puffed out his chest in a comical gesture but never took his right hand from his pocket.

Rooms and closets checked, she resisted the urge to check them a second time. She held Dr. Kimba's arm as they walked to the front door.

"Thank you for a lovely evening." She kissed him on the white stubble of his bearded cheek. "And thank you for walking me in."

"My pleasure. If you remember, mention to Mr. Nicoletti that I will try to reach him tomorrow," he said as he crossed the brick walk. "And replace that porch light."

She closed the door. "It would be nice to have Mr. Nicoletti standing guard at my front door," she said as she headed for the shower.

Dr. Kimba locked the doors to the Volvo and retraced the route he had driven. Two blocks from the yellow-

and-white cottage, he pulled to the curb, turned off the headlights, but kept the engine running. He checked again to be sure the doors were locked. He was in the place where he had seen the gray Suburban.

He looked up and down the street. "Where are you, Charles? What are you up to?" he said to the dark interior of the Volvo, After a few minutes he turned on the headlights and drove home slowly, looking at the cars parked along every street.

Dr. Kimba was relieved to see his own porch light burning brightly as he pulled into the driveway. He turned off the engine and looked at his house. The parlor light was on, as was the light in the upstairs hall. He got out of the car, locked the door, and went inside, holding the derringer firmly in his hand, no longer concealed in his pocket but at his side.

.   .   .

Hidden from the moonlight, Charles Durbin watched the doctor's shadow move from room to room. As he flexed the muscles in his arms and across his back, he felt the power of the night surge through his body.

"You were supposed to help me, not become my enemy," Durbin whispered. "Do you think you can really stop me, old man?" He started to approach the house, then stopped and returned to the shadows. "You will pay for your stupidity, for your failure, but not tonight." He looked at the silhouette in the upstairs window. "Tonight and the next few days will be my gift to you. If you behave yourself."

SEVENTEEN

Len Pandori pulled the cigar from his mouth and blew a smoke ring at the sky.

"Full moon."

"Seven-eighths," Nicoletti said, leaning against Pandori's Jeep in the motel parking lot. "The moon won't be full until tomorrow."

"Whatever." Pandori sent another ring skyward. "So what do you think?"

"About what?"

"About anything—the town, the job offer from the university, about living here."

"How do you like living in Missoula?"

"Love it. And don't answer a question with a question."

"Are you planning on retiring here?"

"Two more years and I'm done. By then, our son will be out of college, and Liz and I are staying right here." Pandori pulled a lighter from his pocket and lit Nicoletti's cigarette. "This is where she grew up, you know."

"Think the Bureau will let you stay here until retirement?" Nicoletti tried his hand at smoke rings around the moon.

"Hell yes. As long as the sheriff or the chief of police or some politician doesn't complain to Washington about me, I'm golden. After I got shot, they paraded me around Capitol Hill as a prop, then shipped me off to Quantico, where I'd lectured every new agent class about the will to survive. I begged them to transfer me back to the field. When they did, I spent years sitting on wiretaps and doing background investigations. Nobody wanted to put a cripple back on the street.

"Finally, five years ago, I got shipped out to the resident office in Billings. The agent who runs that office is an old friend. He lets me work out of Missoula. Basically, I'm a one-man office here. Nice space over in the courthouse. Nothing to complain about."

"How do you get along with Chief Garland?"

"Good. I mean, Pete's a good guy." Pandori relit his cigar, rolling it into the flame of his lighter and puffing on it vigorously. "He runs a good department and has recruited some good guys. We don't always see eye to eye, but I make it my business not to argue with him or contradict him in front of his people."

"That would be a tall order for you, to keep your opinions to yourself." Nicoletti playfully pushed Pandori against the Jeep.

"You're right. Sometimes it's all I can do to keep my fat, Chicago mouth shut, but I do it. Pete Garland is a big man in this city—local boy who made good."

"Big fish in a little pond is more like it."

"And he's going to be a bigger fish after the next election. Next year the sheriff retires, and unless there is a crime wave or major scandal, Garland should have no trouble getting elected." Pandori flicked his cigar ash at Nicoletti.

"Is there enough work here to keep you busy?" he said, brushing the ash from the sleeve of his jacket.

"No. I spend most of my time drinking coffee with the cops and the deputies. Once in a while something will happen, but not often. Hey, but I'm back on the front lines again, and I'm thankful for it every day."

Nicoletti did not comment.

"So what do you think about this place?" Pandori asked again.

"It's interesting."

"Interesting? You've been dying to get out of Washington and leave that law firm investigator's job. Right?"

Nicoletti blew more smoke at the moon.

"What did you tell me? They were buying your life for what, a little over fifty dollars an hour after taxes? You always said you wanted to teach at a college. So here you are. You got a job offer to get in on the ground floor of a new criminal justice program. You could buy a nice piece of land and build the house of your dreams." Pandori grabbed Nicoletti's forearm. "And you just spent the last two hours talking to one of the best-looking women you've ever seen, and all you can say is 'It's interesting'?"

"Two. Two attractive women," Nicoletti said. "Anne and Justine."

"You know what I mean. Don't pretend you didn't see it. Christ, Nico, Marie-Justine is the spitting image of Kristen." Pandori chomped down on his cigar.

"There's a similarity." Nicoletti looked away.

"Hell, Nico, the first time I met her, I almost called her Kristen twice. If Liz hadn't kicked me under the table, I would have."

"How do you know her?"

"Anne brought her over for dinner. Anne and Liz are second cousins. Their grandfathers were brothers. They owned a pretty large spread on the east side of town." Pandori blew smoke against Nicoletti's chest. "The property's been split up over the years between the grandchildren. Liz and her brother have a chunk, and Anne has the rest."

"Anne didn't strike me as a cowgirl."

"Don't let that big-city reporter act and those spiked heels fool you. She's as tough as any rancher." Pandori opened the door of the Jeep. "If you moved here, I could get the sheriff to swear you in as a 'special deputy' and we could work on cases together," he offered as if it had suddenly occurred to him.

"I'll think about it."

"We'll talk later," Pandori said.

He sounded lonely to Nicoletti. "So what about Justine?" Nicoletti asked.

"*Marie*-Justine," Pandori corrected.

"She introduced herself as Justine."

"Whatever. What can I tell you that you didn't already find out? You talked to her for two hours. The Nicoletti I remember could get a confession out of Jack the Ripper in two hours." Pandori got into his Jeep. "I'll call you tomorrow."

"Tomorrow I'm going hiking with Justine," Nicoletti said as he headed for his hotel room.

"You and I are still on for dinner, right?" Pandori yelled across the parking lot. "And her name is *Marie*-Justine."

.   .   .

The message light on the phone in Nicoletti's room was blinking. He dialed for the message.

"Mr. Nicoletti, this is Dr. Kimba. Please call me when you get in. It is eleven o'clock."

Nicoletti looked at his watch. It was 12:15. He decided to call the doctor in the morning.

EIGHTEEN

Occasionally on Sunday afternoons, Dr. Kimba rearranged the artwork in his home. Today was one of those occasions.

From the front hall closet, he pulled out a large canvas in a gilded, antique wood frame. He hung the painting over the fireplace in his office and dusted the frame. He stepped back and marveled at how she had captured the sunlight, pastel colors, and dark green shadows. It was an impressionistic view of a fountain and the surrounding garden at the Broadmoor Hotel in Colorado Springs painted in 1999 by his wife, Helen, on their last vacation, the last trip they took before she became too ill to travel. It was one of two paintings and two sketches she had done of the fountains and gardens. The sketches were done in the summer of 1998, during the middle of the construction of the fountain. He remembered tan workers dragging and lifting amid iron and wood scaffolding, the basic forms just emerging. Somewhere there was the second painting Helen had done from the Broadmoor sketches. He made a mental note to look for that later and perhaps hang it on the opposite wall.

During their forty years of marriage, his Helen had painted or sketched the sights and moments of their lives. The walls, the closets, and the basement of their home were filled with images she had captured in oil and pastel. It was Helen who had established the pattern of rotating the artwork every few months, and he continued the tradition after her death.

At first he found it difficult to take down a painting and put it away. He would be sad to say good-bye to a time and place they had shared. Then he would pull out another painting and it would bring him the joy of a memory long forgotten. Over the years he began to think of the paintings as postcards from Helen. *Remember the time…? Wasn't it lovely when…?* Then he would step back and smile or cry, depending upon how much wine he had had to drink.

Dr. Kimba had converted the small library at the back of his home into an office. It was there that he wrote in the evening and saw patients a few days a week during the afternoon. He didn't have many patients, but there were enough to keep him in touch with the subjects he taught at the university. The room was bright with natural light filtering through the trees along the side of the house. He marveled at the way the sunlight brought out the colors in the painting.

There was a knock on the back door.

"Oh my God," Dr. Kimba muttered. "Is it two already?" His eyes moved to the clock on the mantel below the painting.

"Come in. I'm afraid I'd completely lost track of time."

Charles Durbin shook the doctor's hand firmly and entered the office.

Dr. Kimba pulled his hand free. Something in Durbin's touch sent a chill through the older man's soul.

NINETEEN

The first thirty minutes of the session passed. They faced each other, sitting in leather chairs, separated by a low, mahogany coffee table.

Durbin talked while Dr. Kimba listened and occasionally jotted something in a notebook he held on his lap. Durbin kept his conversation confined to safe and familiar ground: business was good; he was sleeping better, getting to bed early, exercising more, cooking at home more, and eating in restaurants less.

"Did you see the photo of Chief Garland with the governor in yesterday's paper?" Durbin asked. "His wife is a client of mine, you know."

"The governor's wife?"

"No, Jenny Garland."

"I didn't know that."

"Oh yes, one of my first, and a very attractive woman."

The doctor was becoming agitated. He had issues he wanted to discuss, areas he feared to enter but knew needed exploration.

"Charles," Dr. Kimba began, "did we not agree that you would not go out at night alone?"

"Yes. But that was only if I did not have a particular destination in mind and as long as I went directly home when the evening was over." Durbin spoke quietly but stared directly into the doctor's eyes.

"Tell me, Charles, where were you last night?"

"I was home."

"The *truth* or we are done with our sessions. I can't help you if you are not truthful, Charles. I saw your car parked near the university last night."

"I was with a woman." Durbin leaned forward and put his hands together, fingertips touching, pushing against his lips.

"A woman. Any woman, or your Lady A or Lady B?"

"Lady B."

"Well, that must have been a pleasant evening for you." Dr. Kimba loosened his grip on the pen.

"Oh, it was. She met me at the door with a hug and a kiss. Then we went into the kitchen for a glass of wine, and we talked for an hour or more." Durbin stood up and turned, facing the fireplace, his back to the psychiatrist. "We danced and she started kissing me. One thing led to another… She looked lovelier than I had ever seen her look. She wore the prettiest dress—lavender, with a little turquoise star on the zipper. She wore it just for me; it's my favorite." Durbin turned slowly. "Do you want to hear more, Doctor? Do you want the details?"

Kimba looked at the clock on the mantel. Fifteen minutes to go. "If you would like to tell me, go ahead."

Durbin paced the room and talked in a voice that grew huskier as he detailed the intimate experiences of the past evening. Dr. Kimba made a few notes and tried to be casual in his avoidance of Durbin's eyes.

Suddenly, Durbin stopped talking. Dr. Kimba acted as if he were waiting to hear what happened after the lovemaking in the bathroom, but Durbin provided no further details.

"Now that you have committed to Lady B, are we still to refer to her as 'Lady B,' or can we identify her by name?" Dr. Kimba hoped for something, anything that might allow him to warn the unsuspecting woman.

"A gentleman does not reveal the name of his lover."

"And what is to become of Lady A? Is she no longer in your thoughts? After all, not that long ago Lady A was the object of your affection."

"Is this painting new, Doctor?"

"No." He did not want to discuss his wife or her paintings.

"It's the Broadmoor in Colorado Springs, isn't it?"

"Yes," Dr. Kimba said with genuine surprise. "Have you been there?"

"Not for years. Not since I was a child."

"How did you recognize the fountain?"

"I played in it, splashing water on the flowers."

"How old did you say you were then?"

"Oh, no more than seven or eight. I think I was eight."

Dr. Kimba looked at the clock. Five minutes left. "Tell me about your trip to the Broadmoor."

TWENTY

When Nicoletti got back to his hotel he was exhausted, both physically and emotionally. Justine had set a pace for their hike he found difficult to match, hours of walking and talking with little or no rest from either. He found her exhilarating, fascinating. The day had flown by, and it wasn't until he stepped into the dark of his hotel room that he felt like collapsing.

He dialed for his messages. Dr. Kimba had called again. Pandori had also called. Neither of them answered when Nicoletti tried to return their calls. He left them messages promising to call again later. He dropped his clothes on the floor and headed for the shower.

Marie-Justine had asked him if he would like to have dinner with her at her favorite restaurant. He wanted to say yes but remembered his dinner plans with Lenny Pandori and said no. She gave him her phone number and said, "If you change your mind before 5:00, call me."

Somewhere between the shampoo and final rinse, he reached out of the shower and took his watch from the edge of the sink. 5:05. He grabbed a towel and ran to the phone.

Dripping, he searched the pockets of his jacket for the number. He dialed it. No answer. After tapping his wet foot during the answering machine pleasantries, he left a message. "Justine, it's Joseph. It's a little after 5:00. Call me and let me know where you're going for dinner." In his tough-guy voice, he added, "If you don't call, I'll hunt you down."

He grabbed the phonebook from under the nightstand and searched under restaurants for something that looked French. He rubbed his eyes to read the page as water dripped from his face. In small print under the listing for the Chez Margot, he found the description *Modern French Bistro Cuisine.*

She was not inside the restaurant when he arrived. He waited out front, hoping she would show up. At 7:00 he gave up and went inside. It was a long shot that this was the right place. He must have guessed wrong. All he knew at this point was he was starving. Added to the five and a half hours of hiking, the walk to the restaurant made it a full six hours of exercise. His right knee and hip ached.

The room seated about thirty diners comfortably. Most of the tables were occupied by well-dressed couples conversing in the candlelight. Nicoletti felt a little underdressed in jeans, a blue flannel shirt, and a green down vest. Again he scanned the tables for Marie-Justine. She was not there.

The hostess led him to a small table and removed the extra place setting, indicating her choice that he should sit with his back to the front door. Normally, he would always take the seat that allowed him to monitor the comings and goings of any room in which he found himself. He thought about moving, but the throbbing in his knee was subsiding, and the quick delivery of a glass of pinot noir, followed by a pâté with port—Madeira—and a reduction of shallots, settled him down.

The waitress removed the appetizer and replaced it with a salad of seasonal greens with roasted garlic vinaigrette, shaved Jarlsberg, and toasted walnuts. Resigned to eating alone and more than impressed with the food, Nicoletti began to relax.

The chef, a man in his early thirties, nodded as he passed Nicoletti's table. From the entrance area came the quick, clipped tones of an animated conversation in Parisian French. The conversation moved gradually closer until it reached the table directly behind Nicoletti.

"Joseph?" Marie-Justine said.

He turned and started to rise, but she was already at his side, her hand on his shoulder as she bent to kiss his cheek. He was half up and half seated when she introduced him to the restaurant's owners. Awkwardly, he shook their hands as he made his way to his feet.

He pulled the chair out for Marie-Justine. She wore a black, long-sleeved, knit jersey dress, belted in sliver and turquoise, with black leather boots, her hair in the chestnut braid. Her tan skin had a tinge of rose, added by their lengthy hike and enhanced by a silver necklace and earrings. The candlelight accentuated her high cheekbones and danced across her eyes and moist lips. Nicoletti realized it had been a long time since he had been with a woman so beautiful and so full of life. She leaned over and kissed his cheek again.

The owners brought out a bottle of Veuve Clicquot and four glasses to the table. Happily Nicoletti found himself included in the celebration. They toasted to Marie-Justine's continued happiness in her new life, or something of the sort; Nicoletti's French wasn't any good, even before it had become rusty.

The meal was delicious. They shared each other's entrées, passing forks and spoons back and forth, talking and laughing. The waitress offered coffee and dessert. They couldn't. Not another bite. But they did and agreed it was worth it.

"I'm so glad you're here." She reached across the table and took his hand.

The waitress brought the check and Nicoletti placed his credit card on top of it, but Marie-Justine pushed his credit card toward him and replaced it with her own.

"This is my treat," she said.

"No, I can't allow—"

"I insist. I invited you. Even though you said you would not come." She handed her card to the waitress. "If you feel it necessary, you may assert your chivalry by taking me to dinner tomorrow night at your expense."

"I would be honored." He laughed. "Where shall we go?"

"I think it would be appropriate to return to this table for our first real date."

When the waitress returned with the credit card slip for signature, Nicoletti offered Marie-Justine a silver pen from inside his vest.

"This is a pretty pen." She rolled it between her fingers. "What does this say?" She examined the inscription. "*G/S J. Nicoletti*. What is G/S?"

"It means Group Supervisor. It was a gift from another agent when I was promoted many years ago."

"All day long you have prefaced your conversation with 'It was long ago...' or 'It was many years ago...' or 'Back when...' Where is the present in your speech? Is everything in your memory from so long ago?" She signed the bill and handed him the pen. "The past is past, Joseph. Now a new life begins."

The waitress brought a half bottle of champagne and two glasses and handed them to Marie-Justine. "Claude and Joan wish you a happy evening."

Marie-Justine handed the bottle and glasses to Nicoletti. "I must go into the kitchen and say good night. You can come with."

"I'll wait outside," he said.

"Then I will ask Claude for his rabbit sausage recipe for you."

⁎　　⁎　　⁎

Marie-Justine pulled her Mercedes to the curb near the Higgins Street Bridge.

"It is still early. We have cold champagne. I have an idea. Come with me." She got out of the car and walked around to his side. "Come on, Joseph, it's time for a conversation about our new lives."

"New lives?"

"Come now, you are ready for a change, a new beginning. It may not be in Missoula, but by considering it, you have opened yourself up to a world of possibilities."

"And you, what is your new life?"

"A year ago...even a month ago, I would have never approached you as I did at the party the other night. I would have thought it too forward, improper for a lady. My whole life I have done just the right thing. I can tell you it's exhausting."

"Are you telling me you're no longer going to act like a lady?" He placed a hand on her arm and laughed.

"Maybe…but it's more than that. I think I've been afraid…afraid something terrible was going to happen…and believing that if I stayed along a narrow path, I might be able to—"

He wrapped his arm around her shoulders and whispered, "Don't get too wild until you get used to it."

The moon was full and the sky clear. They took the bottle and glasses down a path to the riverside. Nicoletti placed his vest on the ground as a blanket, and they watched the river and listened to its movement.

"See it moving? Always forward." She leaned against his chest. "It cannot go back. If it tries, it will stop. If it stops too long, it dies."

"I get the message, Professor."

"My grandfather's name is Joseph. You would like him. He has a small vineyard in the Vaucluse, east of Avignon. There is a small village down the mountain, with little shops and cafés and a small stone church."

"I was once in a village like that. I used to think I would like to live there," he said.

"You don't think so anymore?"

"I really haven't thought about it in a long time."

"You see, there is something from 'long ago' that you will find in the future." She moved her arm inside his and sipped the champagne.

.   .   .

Marie-Justine drove off, wearing his vest for warmth, leaving Nicoletti standing in the parking lot of his hotel. He was in no mood for sleep. He felt invigorated. He walked along the street, looking at the moon and thinking about the winding path of his life. After years of solitude, having been trained to keep secrets, to keep his distance from friends and enemies alike, he had spent the entire day introducing her to his most intimate thoughts. At times, as they talked, he would pull back, suddenly aware of his abandonment of so many years of careful, calculated conversation. Sensing his unease, she would smile and touch his hand and renew him with the courage to be himself.

Every dream she confided in him, he had dreamed as well. Their beliefs and spiritual paths over the last decades were in unison, connecting them as if they had been together forever and not just acquaintances of a few hours.

TWENTY-ONE

Marie-Justine placed the empty champagne bottle and the two glasses on her kitchen counter. She called Anne, but there was only the recorded voice asking her to leave a message. It was after 11:00. Dinner at the dean's must have been more of a success for Jim than expected, she thought with a smile.

She turned on her computer to send Anne an email, then changed her mind. What she had to say would be better in writing, just as the confessions between them had been written years ago. From the desk, she took note-paper and a pen and sat at the kitchen table. Wrapped in Nicoletti's down vest and the fragrance of his cologne, she began to write.

> *Dearest Anne,*
> *I know we will see each other tomorrow, but I wanted to communicate with you before I go to sleep. I am afraid that after this night ends, I will no longer be able to touch life the way I can at this*

d I *want to share my joy with you, my*
iend, as it exists now.

sterday, I have been consumed with
     and the reality of a man. I know it is
not wise, but wisdom has been our curse as of late.
And, yes, I have probably made a fool of myself, but
what a happy fool.*

*You will likely analyze and dissect this, as is
your way—blame the touch of fall in the air, the
champagne, the final break of the chains that struggled to imprison my soul these last few years—but
please do not. Hear me now, as you would have
when we were young.*

*As you have probably guessed, it is Joseph. We
talked and laughed for hours. I feel more strongly
than yesterday that I have met him before. It is as if
I have known him my whole life, before my life. He
is calm, but with a sense of urgency that is barely
under control. He is a dangerous man. Dangerous
for me to be with, for in those moments, I am lost. I
fear he is burdened by many secrets that would pain
him to reveal. But that is for another time. Tonight,
we opened up to each other and spoke of our hidden dreams, the places we hoped to explore.*

*He knows my life without my saying a word.
He spoke of cities and restaurants that are as much
a part of my past as if it were yesterday. He has
been to the village of my grandfather and eaten in
the bouchons of Lyon. That hazelnut vinaigrette
you love? He has the recipe. He has breakfasted
at Rubino's on Avenue B in Paris. And the little al-
mond pastries that are my favorite? He loves them
too. Perhaps we were there on the same day, at the
same hour, exchanged a greeting. The possibilities
are staggering.*

Everywhere he has gone, I have gone before or after, and now we are here at the same time, in the same place, and it is the magic of which I have always dreamed. As if we were in each other's footsteps our whole lives, one waiting for the other to delay long enough to touch hands. "Turn around." "Wait for me." My soul must have screamed it a dozen times and finally he has heard.

I do not know from which life he has come. Perhaps he was a knight sworn to be my protector. Or a woodcutter who hunted down the rabid wolf so we children could once again play in the forest. He knows that lives pass in time and has heard the messages in the sound of the river and in the wind. That is a part of his life he has hidden for decades, and yet, he felt at ease sharing it with me. He is Brother William of Baskerville, come to bring light to the maze of turrets and hidden passageways of the medieval abbey that has become my life.

Oh, my dearest Anne, I burst at the thought of us spending time with him. Tomorrow I will bring him to you. But I shall bring you this letter first so you can scold me for being such a fool. Let loose your critical eye. He will pass your every test.

I swear, if I live another hundred years, it will be but a moment if I am with him. Time has never seemed so precious.

Yours always,
M-J

She folded the letter and placed it in an envelope, then stood up and hugged his down vest close to her body as she dialed. The hotel operator answered.

"Joseph Nicoletti's room, please."

"I'm sorry, but our internal phone system is out of order. I can't connect you to the guest rooms right now, but I can take a message if you would like."

Marie-Justine hung up and wrote a quick note, placing it in another envelope. On the outside of the envelope she hesitated. How did he spell his last name? Remembering the inscription on his silver-and-gold pen, she reached inside the vest. It was not there. She searched the other pockets, then the kitchen floor, under the table; it was not to be found.

She recalled picking the vest up by the river and had seen a glint of light on the ground. His pen must have fallen from the vest then. She looked at the clock. Just after midnight. She grabbed her keys then stopped. A sudden rush of foreboding flooded into her chest. Her hands trembled.

"No. No more," she said aloud. "I will not be a prisoner to shapeless images laden with fear."

She squeezed the keys and hurried to the Mercedes. The engine raced. If Joseph was not at the hotel she would leave the note, go alone to the river, retrieve his pen, and keep it safe until tomorrow.

·   ·   ·

The gray Suburban came to life and pulled its massive frame down the street. Charles Durbin was out of breath. He had been startled when Marie-Justine suddenly started searching her kitchen. She had been so peaceful while writing at the table. At first he was afraid she had seen him at the window, but when she began pulling the chairs away from the table, he relaxed. Then she bolted from the house to her car. Durbin hardly had time to run down the block to his Suburban before she was racing out of her drive.

"Where are you going, Marie, at this time of night... to meet your new boyfriend? Have you no shame? Don't you know it is dangerous out here in the dark? I can't protect you if you insist on acting so irresponsibly." Durbin became agitated and began to sweat. He picked up a pair of gloves from the front seat and tugged at them until they were on. He followed her to the hotel, watched her enter the lobby, then followed her away.

The Mercedes pulled into a closed gas station near the bridge on Higgins Street where she had parked with Nicoletti. Marie-Justine got out of the car and walked down the path to the river.

Charles Durbin parked a block behind. He took a black dog leash from under the front seat, grabbed a small, green nylon bag and a blanket from the passenger side, and walked to the Higgins Street Bridge.

In the dim light of the bridge lanterns, he examined the contents of the green bag: brush, comb, lipstick, blush, and scissors. He surveyed the street for motion. There was none. He walked quietly down the path to the river where his love was waiting. He needed to meet with her, to reason with her, to stop her before she betrayed their life together.

TWENTY-TWO

After a fitful sleep, Anne Bertone awoke, agitated and ready for a fight. As she bent down to pick up the Monday morning newspaper, coffee spilled from her oversized mug onto the front porch. She licked the side of the dripping mug and used the sports section to absorb the spill. She walked back into the house feeling lightheaded. "Too much wine last night," she mumbled and tossed the paper onto the couch, knocking over a stack of magazines she had no intention of reading.

She glared at the cluttered kitchen table then pushed her notes and research books to the side, clearing a small space for the coffee mug. From under a crumpled towel on the counter, she retrieved a bottle of aspirin. She shook out three of the bitter, chalky pills, popped them into her mouth, and washed them down with a gulp of the black coffee. "Uhhh," she groaned. "Never again."

She dropped onto a bentwood chair next to the amorphous clearing and set the mug on the table with a thud. She tugged at her robe, which had entered into a conspiracy with her nightgown to cut off the blood flow to her right arm. As she pulled the sleeve, the unyielding terry cloth tightened across her back, hampering the movement of her free arm. She shifted in the chair, trying to release the excess material trapped beneath her.

"For Chrissake." She jumped up and tried to tear the enemy sleeve from the shoulder of the robe. Her head throbbed. She pulled her arms from the trap and threw the offending robe into a lifeless lump on the floor. "Piece of shit." She kicked it through the archway into the living room and sat back down. Her nightgown pulled at her chest. "Don't you start with me." She lifted herself up with a slight jump and straightened the garment as best she could before slamming back onto the chair.

She was starting to overheat. On the other side of the kitchen table, her laptop computer hummed quietly; the black screen was awaiting her command to come to life. She took a sip of coffee. Over the rim of the mug she watched the computer screen, a silent reminder of work avoided and unfinished.

"What the hell are you looking at? I'll get to you when I'm damn well ready." She reached across the table and snapped the laptop closed.

"Cigarettes... They're here somewhere." She shuffled the papers and maps. Finally, under a fatuous, self-indulgent, self-published history of rural Montana written by one of Jim's colleagues, she found the remains of a pack of Marlboro Lights.

She surveyed the piles of papers on the table, trying to will her lighter to appear. Then she remembered. She looked at the mound of terry cloth she had just sent flying into the living room. From the pocket of the banished robe, she recovered her lighter. She picked up the robe and draped it carefully over the back of a rocking chair in a gesture of forgiveness.

The smoke made her nauseous, but she refused to put it out. She deserved the punishment. First, because she didn't tell Jim that she was no longer interested in seeing him. She had become annoyed by his weaknesses, real and imagined. The annoyance had led to intolerance for his moody pseudo-classicism. She knew at that point she should dump him, but procrastination and a determination to prove Marie-Justine wrong had kept her hanging on. Now, despite her best efforts, things had progressed to the disgusting, final stage of a bad relationship: indifference.

"I am so glad I never slept with that limp noodle," she said to the burning end of the Marlboro.

Second, because she was stalled in her attempt to finish the final draft of her novel. Her literary agent was already showing impatience with transparent excuses. Recently the agent had stopped trying to understand and had become more aggressive.

"Anne, you've got to buckle down and hammer this out. Your advance was based on the second book being delivered on time." The agent had repeated that message for the third time during Friday's call.

Anne flicked cigarette ashes at the edge of a saucer protruding from beneath a few pages of manuscript notes. She missed. "Shit."

Third, because she had chosen to go with Jim last night out of guilt, instead of having dinner with M-J.

"Anne Bertone, you are a shit best friend."

She crushed the Marlboro in the saucer.

TWENTY-THREE

Police Chief Peter Garland leaned on the hood of his car. It had been a long night, and now he was preparing for a long day. He had been called from his warm bed at 1:15. A bunch of kids got drunk in a trailer park, and their party came to an abrupt end when two of them were stabbed, one fatally.

Garland was back in bed at 6:00. His wife woke him at 8:00.

"The police dispatcher called," Jenny had said. "Some boys found a woman's body along the river by the Higgins Street Bridge."

When he went to bed last night, his Monday had been all planned out: a morning meeting with the chairman of the county's Republican Party, lunch with the deputy mayor, and an afternoon meeting with the county attorney and his good-looking female assistant. Now he was ass deep in a stabbing and two homicides.

Standing with his back to the Higgins Street Bridge Garland looked at his wristwatch; it was ten minutes before noon. He scribbled on an index card.

"Sergeant, send an officer to this address." Garland handed the card to the sergeant. "Have him bring Anne Bertone to my office. And tell the officer not to discuss this killing with Miss Bertone. Just have him tell her I need to talk with her, nothing more than that. I also want two officers sent to the victim's home." He handed another index card to the sergeant. "Tell them to secure the residence from the outside. Don't go in, and don't touch anything."

"Ten-four, Chief." Sergeant Tom Sheppard put one of the cards in his pocket. "I'll grab one of the guys and head over to the victim's residence and secure it myself."

"Thanks, Tom," Garland said. "I'll join you as soon as I can."

The paramedics loaded the body into the ambulance. Pete Garland watched as the detectives tagged plastic evidence bags and dropped them into cardboard boxes in the trunk of their car. He pulled up next to the detectives' vehicle and rolled down his window.

"In addition to the officers assigned here, leave a man on the other side of the bridge to keep tabs on anyone showing too much interest from that side of the river and anyone who crosses the bridge more than once and shows any interest in the crime scene." Chief Garland pointed at the walkway along the bridge. "And let's expand the area inside the tape. I want a larger crime scene protected. We can always scale it back later." He waited for the detectives to acknowledge his instructions. They nodded. "If we get a bad feeling about someone, I want him identified." Garland took a sip of cold coffee from the Thermos he had placed in the car when he headed out to the trailer park eleven hours ago. "I also want the physical evidence sorted out as soon as possible. Don't wait for a formal report; brief me verbally. And have the Mercedes towed to the station for storage."

"Ya know, Chief," Detective Reichert said, "we could use some help on this one." He lowered his voice. "Maybe you could borrow a few investigators from the sheriff's office, you know, just until we get this thing kinda sorted out."

"Just take your time and follow procedure. If you need help, we'll discuss it later." Garland started to drive off, but stopped. "The state police crime scene boys weren't enough help?"

"Oh yeah, they were great, but now we need to start runnin' down leads. A few extra guys could speed things up a bit," Reichert said.

"I'll ask the sheriff to send over a few deputies to take over security of the scene. That'll free up our officers to help you out. Also, I called and asked Sergeant Bennigan to bring his bloodhound, Duke, over here and work the scene. Make sure he gets whatever he needs."

"We might wanna consider setting up surveillance at the victim's house to get tag numbers of passing cars and maybe pull over and ID anyone who slows down in front," Reichert said.

"I'll think about that. You just concentrate on the scene here for now."

The chief's car pulled away, and the two detectives shook their heads.

"Is there anything else? How about we repaint the jail while we're at it?" Reichert said, slamming the trunk lid shut. "Expand the crime scene." He snapped off a pair of latex gloves. "Now that everybody and his mother has been milling around down there, he wants to rope it all in. We'll be pickin' up cigarette butts and hair and photographin' boot prints till next summer."

"What do you want me to do?" the younger detective asked.

"You heard the son of a bitch. Grab that crime scene tape and close off another fifty feet in every direction."

"You think that will be large enough?"

"Don't make me shoot you, kid."

Reichert punched in a number on his cell phone. The call was picked up on the second ring. "Pandori, this is Reichert. Anybody call you yet?... No, not about the stabbings. About the woman found by the river.... Well, pack your ass up and meet me on the south side of the Higgins Street Bridge.... Now. Unless it's going to interrupt your golf game, we got a mess here and I need your input."

TWENTY-FOUR

Pandori closed his cell phone and pushed away from the table. "Sorry, guys, I got to go."

"What do you want me to do when your sandwich comes?" Nicoletti asked.

"Just tell them to wrap it up. I'll stop by later and pick it up." Pandori headed out the door.

Nicoletti opened a small bag of chips and offered one to Dr. Kimba. "So tell me, Doctor, what is it that you think I can help you with?"

"I have been treating a patient who claims to have a compulsive behavioral disorder."

"Claims?" Nicoletti munched on a chip.

"Well, that's the problem. I'm beginning to question the information he has provided to me during our sessions. He claims to have an uncontrollable urge toward voyeurism." Dr. Kimba looked around the delicatessen and lowered his voice. "He can't stop himself from looking into people's windows at night."

"How old is he?"

"Thirty-five, with a life full of horrible stories—abandoned by an abusive father, an alcoholic mother who engaged in small-town prostitution and took on a series of male companions who served up varying degrees of abuse, both physical and mental, to both mother and child."

"Charming."

"There are all sorts of stories he recalled during our sessions. Before he was a teenager, he became his mother's caretaker, cooking, cleaning, and doing the rest of the domestic chores."

The waitress delivered three red plastic baskets to the table. "What happened to Agent Pandori?" she asked.

"He had to get back to work. Can you wrap his up and hold it for him? He said he'd be back later to pick it up," Nicoletti said. "Just put it on my check."

"Do you want Dr. Kimba's lunch on there too?"

"Yes, please." Nicoletti raised his hand to quell the doctor's objection. The waitress walked away and Nicoletti motioned in her direction. "Does she know everyone in town?"

"Only the celebrities."

"So your patient is a slave to circumstance. Does he get a break?"

"No, from a developmental perspective, things get worse. When he was a boy, a woman in her thirties moved in next door. He described her as very 'exotic' and 'beautiful,' but to what degree an adolescent is capable of making such evaluations… In any case, he recalled that she dressed provocatively, and he would watch her from his bedroom window. As time went on, he crept around her house at night and was rewarded for his efforts by being able to observe her in various stages of undress."

"Do you want the ketchup or the mustard?" Nicoletti took a bite of his corned beef sandwich and held up the condiments.

"Mustard, yes, thank you." Dr. Kimba swabbed the mustard on his liverwurst with onion on rye. "So one morning, she caught him peeking into her bedroom and brought him into the house. He told her his mother was passed out with a hangover, so she offered him pancakes and bacon.

"Breakfast at the exotic neighbor's house became a Saturday morning ritual. The catch is that, while he sat in the kitchen waiting for breakfast, she paraded around in front of him wearing very little clothing, and what she did wear was more or less see-through." Dr. Kimba bit into his sandwich, then wiped the mustard from the corner of his mouth.

"By the age of twelve, the neighbor had introduced him to sex. At first she made him sit on a chair in her bedroom while she performed stripteases followed by masturbation. Not long thereafter, he was subjected to quite an array of what one would call perversions. In particular, he said she enjoyed having him stand next to the bed and pull a scarf tightly around her neck as she lay facedown. She would then, well, you know… an autoerotic asphyxiation." Kimba sipped his iced tea.

"Then, as suddenly as she had arrived, she moved away, leaving him a parting gift: a paper bag containing unwashed undergarments."

"I suppose a pocket watch was too expensive."

"Yes, ha, quite good." Dr. Kimba laughed and took another drink of iced tea.

"The rest of his stories involve trouble in high school, the torture of being a loner, a series of failed relationships with the opposite sex, more voyeurism, and the like. Among the dozens of recollections he confided in me, there was one story that caught my attention, or rather, it stopped me cold and has caused me to question everything he has said. It involved a girl his age who lived down the street from his boyhood home. He was in high school at the time. His description of her house and their relationship sounded very familiar to me." He put down his sandwich and leaned both elbows on the table. "Are you familiar with the name Lee Kramer?"

"Wasn't he the Louisville pharmacist who selected his victims from his customer list? Mostly women who had prescriptions for birth control pills. Five known kills," Nicoletti said.

"Precisely." Dr. Kimba took a bite of the liverwurst that was escaping the side of the bread. "I had read Kramer's biography several years ago. After the session ended, I rummaged through some boxes stored in the basement and found the book. I thumbed through it and found the part where he described his first sexual assault. It matched the story my patient had just related. The two versions were virtually identical. The description of the girl, her family, her home...Everything was the same, right down to the wrought iron fence in her yard. The only difference between the two stories was that my patient claimed he never assaulted the girl, only peered in her windows at night, whereas in Kramer's version, the girl was beaten, sodomized, and strangled." He put his sandwich into the red plastic basket and pushed it away. "So, what do you think?"

TWENTY-FIVE

"First of all, let's get something straight: I am no expert in this kind of thing," Nicoletti said.

"Don't be modest. I've read your journal articles on the subject. Your observations and criticisms of several investigations into this type of personality were very insightful."

"Those articles were based on cases that were closed. The actual work had been done by dozens of detectives long before I read the files. And many of the suggestions to correct the approach to the investigation of serial offenders came from detectives I interviewed, who, if you recall, were given adequate credit for their comments in the footnotes."

"What about the Miami Grove killer? You made that case yourself."

"That was luck. I was watching a money courier who was working for a drug smuggler. The killer selected her as a target and was watching her too. I was lucky to see him and figure out what he was doing before he saw me."

"In my reading of the case, it seemed a bit more complicated than that. You also caught that child murderer in Maryland a few years ago. Was that luck too?"

"More or less. I spotted him at the funeral of one of his victims."

"The dead child was the daughter of a policeman, and as I recall, at the time of the funeral, no one knew what the murderer looked like. So how did you know?"

"I didn't know, not at first."

"Weren't there dozens of officers at the cemetery?"

"Hundreds."

"And if my readings are accurate, at those occasions, there are teams of detectives assigned to look for people who are acting in a suspicious manner. So how is it that among all those trained eyes, you alone spotted the killer?"

"Motion."

"Excuse me?"

"Motion...the flow. You know the expression 'Go with the flow?' Well, he didn't."

"I'm not sure I understand..."

"Everything has a rhythm. Individuals, streets, neighborhoods, sections of entire cities...They all have their own tempo. That's why when you visit a strange city, you feel a little awkward at first. You are either walking too fast or too slow. People bump into you. They crowd against you at the crosswalk, lose patience with your driving, any number of things. That's because you are out of sync with the rhythm, the flow of the city."

"And that is how you spot these killers?"

"Basically, yes. Once you understand the patterns of local behavior, anyone who is out of sync will stand out as clearly as if they were covered in yellow paint."

"And in the Maryland case?"

"He drifted, falling farther and farther back in the crowd that was moving to the graveside. Before the service was over, he started to walk away. My partner and I followed him to a bus stop. He got off a few blocks later and got into a car. We got the tag number and went to his home.

"He was living with his grandmother, who allowed us into his room. Among the items on his dresser was a necklace—a Miraculous Medal, gold, with a silver Virgin Mary set in the center of a blue enamel background. The victim had worn one that was not recovered with her body. I called the detective who had the case and we waited for the grandson to return home.

"Twenty minutes after he walked in the door, he confessed. That's all there was to it."

"I won't contradict your modest rendition," Dr. Kimba said, "but in my study of the subject, very few detectives ever actually work on serial murder investigations. And of those who do, only a tiny fraction actually capture the killer. You, my modest friend, have captured two, which by my calculation, puts you in an exclusive club having only one member.

TWENTY-SIX

Dr. Kimba squeezed another lemon into his tea. "So, what do you think about my patient?"

"From the basic pattern you described, it is highly unlikely that at the age of thirty-five your guy has never developed beyond the 'Peeping Tom' stage, unless he spent the last decade in prison. That might account for an arrested development in his predatory pattern."

"I never thought of that." Dr. Kimba ran his bony fingers through his wild hair.

"Does he travel?"

"No, not that I know of. He runs a business in town."

"Well, he couldn't have been killing women for the last fifteen years in a town this size without getting caught." Nicoletti leaned back.

"Oh, he's not from here. He moved to Missoula about a year ago, just before I started seeing him as a patient."

"Where's he from?"

"I don't know. But I caught him in a lie yesterday afternoon. He was looking at my wife's painting of a fountain and claimed to have played in it when he was a small child."

"And the fountain doesn't exist? Your wife made it up?" Nicoletti guessed.

"No, it's quite real, only it was built in 1999. It was part of a new addition to the Broadmoor Hotel in Colorado Springs."

"Well, Doc, maybe he's lying to you about everything and is willing to pay you just to listen to him tell stories about serial killers, or he's telling you some kind of the truth mixed in with fantasy. In either case, you've got yourself a certifiable whacko."

"The reason I'm telling you all this is because I would like you to review his file with me. You could help me spot the vignettes that are derived from the published lives of known killers. Once the fraudulent passages are deleted, the story that is left should be close to his true reality, and I might have a better understanding of how to help him."

"Doesn't that violate your doctor–patient relationship?" Nicoletti asked.

"I'm an MD, a psychiatrist, and you're a criminologist. I view it as an academic inquiry designed to enhance the understanding of the dangerous mind. As long as I don't reveal his identity to you, there is no problem about which I am concerned."

"Whatever you say, Doc." Nicoletti thought for a moment. "Is this patient currently involved in any relationships? Does he claim to have any women in his crappy life?"

"Actually, he said he's been trying to decide between two women. He describes both of them as 'exotic and aristocratic.' Apparently, last Saturday night, he finally settled on one. He told me about their evening together."

"Sounds like a bunch of crap," Nicoletti mumbled. "When did he tell you this?"

"It was during his regular appointment yesterday afternoon. He went into great detail, full of specifics—they were at her home, there was a glass vase full of fresh cut flowers by the front door, she wore a lavender dress with a turquoise star attached to the zipper, they made love in the bathroom. He described how erotic it was to watch their shadows cast upon the tile wall by a nightlight that was plugged in just above the baseboard." Dr. Kimba wiped his chin with the back of his hand. "It was all very graphic, I must say."

Nicoletti exhaled deeply and held the doctor's stare. "If he's a killer, he's getting close to making his move. Maybe he has been debating between two women, and now he has chosen one to be his victim. What's worse is that it sounds like he's already familiar with the interior of her home. That means she knows him and maybe trusts him, or he has a way of entering her home without her knowledge. Either way, it's not good." Nicoletti leaned back in his chair. "Or, it could all be bullshit."

"What if it is not and he is telling some twisted version of the truth?" Dr. Kimba asked.

"Then the first thing to do is to take out an ad in tomorrow's paper:

Are you a woman living alone?
Do you have a glass vase by your front door?
Did you wear a lavender dress Saturday?
Does it have a turquoise star attached to the zipper?
If the answer to these questions is YES:
Run to the nearest police station!

"That should do it, don't you think?"

"I don't regard this as a laughing matter, Mr. Nicoletti."

"Neither do I, Doc. But if we could publish it, I would. And I'll go you one better: after we place the ad, you take me to this lunatic's house and help me find the box of dirt he sleeps in. I'll personally drive a wooden stake through his heart."

Dr. Kimba smiled and shook his head. "Will you help me go over the file tonight?"

"I'll be there. How's seven sound?" Nicoletti picked up the check and they walked to the cashier. "Wait, Doc, I can't make it tonight. I have a previous commitment."

"I cannot stress the urgency I feel in this matter. Could you possibly rearrange your schedule?" He grasped Nicoletti's arm.

"I've got a dinner date with Justine, Marie-Justine. I can't break it. I promised her."

"Well, tomorrow then, after your lecture. How about one o'clock? I'll make us lunch."

"Done." Nicoletti took his change from the cashier and placed it on the table next to the red baskets.

"I must tell you, I am relieved that you will be with Marie-Justine. She is a wonderful woman. If I were thirty years younger, I'd give you a run for your money with that one."

Nicoletti patted the doctor on the back as they stepped into the street. The doctor paused and looked seriously at Nicoletti.

"I enjoyed your lecture this morning very much. I wish it had been on serial murder, but I guess the parallel

development of community policing in various socioeco-
nomic sectors of major cities can be just as interesting."

"Doc, are you fuckin' with me?"

"See you tomorrow for lunch. Give my best to
Marie-Justine. Bon appétit."

TWENTY-SEVEN

In a coffee shop across the street, Charles Durbin stopped at a table near the door where a young police officer was drinking from a large red mug.

"How's it going, Bill?" Durbin was holding a Styrofoam cup and a cheese Danish.

"Hey, Charlie, what's going on?"

"Not much. Just staying busy. How about you? Catching any crooks?"

"I wish."

"Things slow?"

"Hell no, the shit really hit the fan today."

"What's going on?" Durbin asked casually.

"Last night there was a double stabbing. One of the poor bastards died at the scene."

"Yeah, I think I heard that on the radio this morning."

"And this morning"—the officer lowered his voice— "they found a dead woman near the Higgins Street Bridge. They say it looks like she was murdered."

Durbin sat down next to the officer and leaned toward him, speaking softly. "Murdered? Did you see her?"

"No, no such luck. I'm assigned as security for some bullshit law enforcement conference over at the university. Bunch of fancy-ass experts lecturing on a lot of crap. Figures, the one time something really good happens, I'm sitting on my ass doing nothing."

Durbin looked out the window as Dr. Kimba walked out of the deli across the street accompanied by a larger man.

"Do you know who that guy is with Dr. Kimba?" Durbin kept a casual tone in his voice.

"Yeah, his name is Nicoletti. He's some big-time investigator from Washington, DC, another fancy expert lecturing at the conference."

Durbin waited for Kimba and Nicoletti to go their separate ways.

"Well, Bill, I'd better get back to work. Good luck on those cases."

Half a block from the coffee shop, Durbin threw the pastry and coffee away as he followed Nicoletti down the street.

TWENTY-EIGHT

Chief Garland sat behind his desk, looking at the twisting leaves on the tree outside his office window. On the other side of the desk, Deputy Chief McKay was lighting his pipe.

"What the hell is happening to this town?" Garland said. "Two murders and a maiming in one night would have been unthinkable when I joined the department fifteen years ago. No one would have believed it, much less known what to do about it."

"Well, times change. Now we've got established procedure to follow," McKay said. "You have to admit we've been lucky. The few murders we've had in Missoula were solved pretty quickly."

"Yeah, by finding the killer still hanging around in the same room as the corpse." Garland put his feet on the windowsill.

"Not always. There have been a few 'whodunits' over the last few years."

"Name one."

"What about the body they found out east behind the truck stop?"

"That was solved by the sheriff's office and the state police."

"Yeah, but we helped with the arrest." McKay struck another match and sucked on his pipe, sending a blue cloud across the desk.

A female officer knocked on Garland's open door. "Chief, Sheriff Rogers is on line two," she said.

"Tell him I'll call him back."

"Better take the call and get it over with," McKay advised.

"Okay, I'll pick it up," Garland said to the officer. Then to McKay he said, "You know what he wants. He'd just love it if we asked for help so he could send Doug Martin over to solve this case." Garland stood up. "Then Martin could throw it in my face next November."

"Rogers is retiring; he's got no agenda. He's already said that he believes either you or Martin would make a good sheriff."

"That's not the kind of endorsement I find very comforting." Garland picked up the phone and punched the button for line two. "Hey, Bob, how ya doing?... Things are a little hectic here right now, I can tell you that... We've already got a confession on the stabbing. The boys are just cleaning it up." Garland shrugged his shoulders at McKay. "Well, that one is gonna be a bit tougher... No, no leads yet, but we haven't had a chance to take a good look at the evidence... I appreciate that, Sheriff... I will... No, I won't hesitate. I'll brief you once I get some info worth talking about... Okay, thanks again." He hung up the phone.

"Very cordial, Pete," McKay said. "I can hear ol' Doug Martin now: 'They're gonna screw it up, Sheriff, I guarantee it.'"

"Well, Doug Martin's wrong. We're not gonna screw up anything. We'll find Marie-Justine's killer and nail his balls to the barn door."

Garland's private line rang. He looked at the phone then at McKay, who was getting up to leave. Garland waited for McKay to close the door before he answered the phone.

Anne Bertone's voice was harsh. "Pete, what the hell is going on? Why do you want to see me? And why did you send an officer over here? You know where I live."

"I sent him to bring you down to my office." Garland took a deep breath.

"He told me that. What do you want?"

"I want you to come down here so I can discuss something with you." Garland leaned on his desk and rubbed his right hand up and down the side of his face and across the back of his neck.

"I'm not going anywhere unless you tell me what the hell this is all about."

"Annie, for once in your stubborn life, will you just do what you are told and stop arguing?"

"Fuck you, Pete. Tell me, or I'm not coming."

"It's Marie-Justine. There's been an accident." He slumped in his chair.

"Is she all right? Is she in the hospital?"

"Just get down here and I'll explain."

TWENTY-NINE

The midday sun washed across the desk and touched the legs of the crying woman. Chief Garland closed the door to his office, leaving Anne Bertone alone in a chair, her arms wrapped around her legs, pulling them against her chest, trying to understand that her closest friend had been murdered.

There was no need for Anne to identify the body; Garland had already taken care of that. He walked down the hall and into the briefing room. Several uniformed officers and all four of the department's detectives were already seated. Reichert stood at the front of room. Garland sat near the back, next to Lenny Pandori.

"Here's what we got, Chief," Detective Reichert began. "Victim's been identified as Marie-Justine Cantrell, white female, forty-two years of age, resides at— Sorry, you knew the victim." Reichert paused as he handed some papers to Garland. "Here's the bio sheet."

Garland set the papers face down on the desk. He looked at Reichert, who was standing in front of a blackboard, and nodded for him to continue.

"We've got Polaroid photos and some digitals already printed out." He taped a few to the blackboard and set the rest on the desk in front of him. "They took some 35-millimeter shots that won't be ready until later."

The officers passed the photographs they were handed as Reichert continued.

"The victim was most likely attacked from behind. Some type of webbed belt, or possibly a horse lead, was placed around her neck. The marks indicate the belt-like item was an inch wide and about a quarter of an inch thick with a tightly woven fiber, probably nylon. It was pulled tight at the back of her neck. Looks like she was pulled to the ground from behind. There was dirt on her back, as well as rock and twig abrasions on her palms and the back of her boots."

He pointed to a Polaroid. "There also was dirt and a slight tear on the right elbow of her dress. The victim had additional abrasions on her cheeks and nose. The medical examiner said she may have been held facedown in the dirt for the kill, but everything is subject to change after—"

"Detective Reichert," Chief Garland interrupted, "we all know this information is very preliminary. I asked for this briefing so that everyone working the case would have a general idea of what we're dealing with. Don't bother to qualify your statements. Just tell us what we've got. Tell us what you think—your best guess."

"Sure, Chief." Mike Reichert walked to a sketch he had taped to the blackboard. "You all have a copy of this in the packets I gave you." He continued while they shuffled their papers. "The initial attack occurred here." He pointed to the sketch. "The victim was then carried to a wooded area and laid out on pine needles here"—he pointed—"where two kids, doing a little fishing before school, found her this morning just before six. We talked it over with Agent Pandori and decided that the body was staged in the position we found it, to accommodate the killer's fantasy. Although the victim was not wearing any underwear when we recovered the body, there was no evidence of vaginal or anal penetration."

Reichert handed out a second series of photographs. "You'll notice her hair was combed to one side, held in place by a large silver comb." He held up an evidence bag containing the comb. "It is plastic and could have been purchased anywhere.

"Around her neck is a red velvet ribbon, fashioned as a choker and tied at the back. Once the ribbon was removed, the indentation and abrasions caused by the ligature were evident."

Garland spoke. "According to information received, the hairstyle, the makeup, the red choker, and the absence of underpants are all inconsistent with the victim's normal behavior."

"Thanks, Chief. Everyone got that?" Reichert continued. "We found some pine needles in her hair, underneath where it's combed over. The ME also found dirt and an abrasion under the makeup on her cheek."

"What?" Garland said, dropping the photographs on the table.

"The medical examiner thinks the killer combed her hair and put the makeup on her after the kill." Detective Reichert stopped and stared at the doorway.

Garland followed his gaze and saw Anne Bertone, hands at her side, defenseless against Reichert's description of the events that Garland knew were slashing at her mind and body.

"Anne, you can wait in my office," Garland said.

"I'm fine here, Peter. Detective, please continue."

"Chief?" Reichert asked.

"Go ahead, Mike," Garland said, looking at Anne.

"We believe we found the area of the initial attack," Reichert continued. "Victim's car keys were on the ground and the rocks and dirt were disturbed like there had been a brief scuffle of some sort."

Lenny Pandori interjected. "We had Bennigan's bloodhound, Duke, work the area. He tried to scent off the red velvet ribbon, which we believe was tied behind the victim's neck by the killer. After a bit of circling, he pulled Bennigan up the hill to the street then lost the scent about half a block away."

"If he ever had the scent," Reichert added. "We also found this silver-and-gold pen off to the side of the attack area." He held up an evidence bag containing the pen. "It's engraved 'G/S J. Nicoletti.'"

Garland looked at Pandori. They both looked at Anne and then again at each other. Meanwhile, Reichert kept on talking.

"There was a green down vest near the body, with two drops of blood and a large blood smear on it." Reichert held up another bag. "Size double extra large, so probably not the victim's. In the pocket of the vest was a business card for the Chez Margot over on South Orange; we're preserving the card for prints. I sent a uniformed officer to the restaurant owners' house to ask if they remember the victim or the vest."

"She went to dinner there last night. The owners are friends of hers," Anne Bertone said from the doorway. "I was supposed to go with her." She began to shake. "But I..."

Garland walked over to Anne, put his arm around her shoulders, and escorted her out of the room.

THIRTY

Anne Bertone sat at the kitchen table in the yellow-and-white cottage. Holding back tears, she read the last letter Marie-Justine had written. Around her, detectives and laboratory technicians rummaged through the small house, looking for a hint of a killer.

"We're going to need to keep that letter, Anne," Chief Garland said as he touched her shoulder.

"I know." Anne looked at the delicate penmanship on the ivory page and the latex gloves that encased her hands. They somehow kept her from really feeling connected to Marie-Justine's letter. Gloves and a pair of cotton mesh boots pulled over her shoes were her part of the bargain with Garland for being allowed to enter the crime scene. Anne resented the strangers moving from room to room and touching the personal possessions that had been Marie-Justine's.

She folded the letter, slid it back into the envelope, and dropped it into the plastic evidence bag. She handed the bag to Garland.

"I've got to notify next of kin," Garland said. "Her father lives in Europe somewhere and her husband is in California, right?"

"Geneva. Her father lives in Geneva. But he is in New York at a World Health Organization meeting at the United Nations this week."

"There's a New York number here on this pad. We can try that," Garland said, handing the pad to Anne.

"Her ex-husband lives in Santa Monica. I've got his number in my purse." She took the pad from Garland. "I'll call them both."

"Tell them I'll call tomorrow with an official follow-up," Garland said. Then, as an afterthought, he said, "Actually, give me the number for the ex-husband. I want to hear his reaction to the news. You call the father. And use one of the department cell phones. They haven't dusted the home phones for prints yet."

Standing on the patio of Marie-Justine's yellow-and-white house, Anne clutched the cell phone as she waited for the operator at the Waldorf Astoria Hotel in New York to connect her to Dr. Louis Junot's suite, searching for the words to tell a father his only child was dead.

A few minutes later it was done. When her tears subsided, she walked back into the kitchen and heard Chief Garland issuing orders.

"And I want the latent prints lifted from the champagne bottle, the two glasses, and every surface you can find in the house before you guys go home tonight." Garland acknowledged Anne, then turned to address the lead detective. "Reichert, the victim's letter talked about a guy named Joseph, so let's make the quantum leap and assume that the 'J. Nicoletti' on the pen you found is Joseph Nicoletti. Call Lenny Pandori and find out where Nicoletti is staying."

"You want someone to pick this Nicoletti guy up?" Reichert asked.

"Not yet. Let's wait until after we're done here and I've had a chance to review the evidence again. And remind Pandori not to contact Nicoletti until I tell him to." Garland turned to Anne. "Did you speak to the father?"

"He's booking a flight from New York to Missoula. He is going to try to get in tonight, but in any event, he'll be here tomorrow. He will call me when he gets in."

"Bring him to my office as soon as he gets here. I talked to the husband. He acted shocked. Said he was at a dinner party last night until after eleven. Claimed fifteen people could alibi him and provided the name of a woman who can attest to his being at home the rest of the night. How long have they been divorced?"

"Officially? About 48 hours."

"He didn't waste any time getting back into the swing of things."

"M-J and the eminent Dr. David Cantrell have been separated for several years. But he was in the swing of things for a good while before that," Anne said.

"I'm going to need whatever details you have about their relationship, as well as the terms of the divorce and Dr. Cantrell's attitude toward the whole thing."

"Not now, Pete. I'm really not up to it. I'd just like to go home." Anne could feel the tears fill her eyes. Her throat tightened as she picked up a photograph in a silver frame from the bookshelf above the desk. "This is M-J and me on a sailboat off the coast of St. Martin. It was taken during spring break when we were sophomores in college," she said to Garland, who wasn't listening.

"What did the neighbor say?" Garland asked one of the officers.

"Neighbor's name is Dorothy Jaeger. She said she was raking her yard Saturday afternoon. About three o'clock, she came around the corner of her house and saw a man looking through the hedge at the victim, who was sitting on the patio."

"Did she have a description?"

"Yeah, said that he was a white male, about fifty, with salt-and-pepper hair. A big guy."

"How big?"

"She just kept saying 'big.' But, Chief, this lady is in her eighties and is no more than four foot eleven. She said he was bigger than me and 'looked like he could kick my ass.' Those were her words, Chief, not mine."

"You got a full description, clothing and all?"

"Yes, sir. She said the guy had claimed that he tripped on the uneven sidewalk and ended up in the bushes, but the old lady said there was no doubt he was checking out the victim. The guy said he was going to be a professor at the university."

"It was Nicoletti," Anne Bertone said. "I was on the phone with M-J when all that was going on."

"Did Marie-Justine know him then?" Garland said.

"No, but we met him Saturday night at Dean Hawkins' party. Remember?"

Garland looked back at the officer. "Go back to Mrs. Jaeger. See if she can remember anything else and tell her we will want to talk to her again real soon. Then help Sergeant Sheppard with the other interviews."

Garland started to walk back into the kitchen, but the young officer was still standing in the living room.

"Was there something else, Officer?"

"No, sir."

"Then get back out there and keep digging." Garland waited a beat, then said, "And good job with the old lady."

The officer smiled and walked past Anne, who was beginning to realize that while she was racked with questions, memories, and pain, these men were systematically participating in a separate reality. They were immersed in an atmosphere of power, position, procedure, and ambition, each one in pursuit of the killer for his own reason.

"Pete, take me home."

"Are you sure there is nothing missing? Nothing out of place?" Garland asked. "Nothing that's here now that shouldn't be?"

"I've told you no. Nothing." She found it difficult to catch her breath. "I need to go home. Now."

THIRTY-ONE

Nicoletti walked into the motel lobby to get a newspaper. The headline in the local paper read: FATAL STABBING AT NORTHWAY TRAILER PARK. He decided against the purchase. He was in too good a mood to deal with local tragedies.

"Good afternoon, Mr. Nicoletti," the desk clerk said. "I've got some messages for you—one from late last night and two from early this morning."

"I don't recall seeing the message light on my phone," Nicoletti said.

"We've been having some phone system problems since the remodeling began." The clerk handed the pink message slips to Nicoletti. "But everything is working now."

There were three messages, two instructing him to call his office. He threw them away. The third was in a sealed envelope. On the outside, his name was written in a feminine hand.

"When was this dropped off?" he asked the clerk.

"Sometime last night, before I came on shift this morning."

Nicoletti headed across the parking lot toward his motel room and pulled the note from the envelope. He read it several times:

Monday night is a lifetime away
I will be waiting for you
As I have my whole life

—Justine

Nicoletti turned his face to the sunlight and took a deep breath. He was elated. She was all he could think about.

Justine had come to him in a dream last night. She had taken him to a clearing in a forest, and they had walked along a path above a beautiful hillside vineyard. He remembered her holding his hand and calling to a large white dog that appeared from nowhere to walk by her side.

They had sat by a stone marker, and he felt a sense of warmth, of peace and tranquility among the vines. In the distance, he saw a stone and timber cottage. From the covered porch, two women called to her. She let go of his hand, and he was alone.

He had followed the path toward the cottage, the dog at his heels. Thunderclouds rolled over the mountain and a cold rain struck his face.

He awoke in his hotel room, and for a frightful moment, he had questioned if Justine existed at all. The digital glare from the clock radio told him it was 1:00 A.M., and he fell back to sleep.

Now, in the afternoon light, he held her message and was glad. She was not a dream. She was real and he wanted to fill his life with her. His first impulse was to drive to her home and take her in his arms. But he had no car. He could take a cab to her house. He could walk. What if she wasn't home? He could wait on her front steps, but for how long?

No, he would not go. She had his number and knew where he was. If she wanted to see him before their dinner date, she would call. For once in his life, he would be patient and wait.

He called his office in Washington, DC, from his room and left a message for the lead defense attorney assigned to the case he was working on.

He poured a glass of wine, opened his window and door, and felt the flow of fresh air fill the room. He took an address book from his briefcase and called a Colorado number for Thomas Marley.

"Hello?" The woman's voice was cheerful and clear.

"Kate, how are you?" Nicoletti said.

"Hey, Uncle Nico. We're great."

"And the kids?"

"Perfect. Just wonderful," Kate Marley said.

"I saw your mother last week. She is looking very well."

"I know. She told me you guys went to dinner with her new boyfriend. She said you're doing great and looking more handsome than ever."

"She's full of it."

"How's her new beau? What's the scoop?"

"He seemed nice, polite, well-dressed. A little too liberal for me. Definitely not as stuffy as that last guy who tried to talk her into getting married."

"Oh, poor Dr. James. I felt so bad for him. He was really crazy about Mom."

"Well, your mother had already been married to the best guy in the world. Your dad is a tough act to follow."

The phone was silent, and Nicoletti felt a pain in his heart for the young woman on the other end of the line.

"I know," Kate finally said. "But Dad's been gone now for almost ten years. I just wish Mom would find someone to share her life with."

"Don't worry about your mother. She knows what she's doing."

"And what about you? When are you going to slow down and let lightning strike?"

"I think I'm a little too old for lightning."

"That's not true. Mom always says you're one of the most eligible bachelors she can think of, and I must admit, I agree."

"Hey, I called to talk to your husband about the thirty-five acres north of Monument that Kristen and I bought a few years back."

"That little ranch on the lake? You're finally going to leave DC, and move out here?"

"That was your Aunt Kristen's dream. I'm not so sure there would be any point in doing it without her. I'm just checking a few things out, considering my options. I was thinking of putting the land on the market, maybe selling the house in DC, and doing some traveling. I've been thinking I might even move to France," Nicoletti said.

"And buy that vineyard you and Dad always talked about? Are you sure there isn't a little lightning or a miracle worker to bring you around to this?"

"No one is bringing me around to anything. I've just started thinking about opening doors I closed long ago. Now put your DEA-agent husband on the phone. And don't say anything to your mother. I'm just thinking of making some changes. I haven't decided anything yet."

After ten minutes of conversation, Nicoletti hung up the phone and poured another glass of wine. He loosened his tie, sat on the bed, leaned back, propped his head on the pillow, and fell asleep.

At three o'clock, he awoke to the sound of someone knocking on the door and calling his name. He opened the door and saw two uniformed police officers.

"Mr. Joseph Nicoletti, I'm Sergeant Tom Sheppard. Chief Garland would like to talk to you at police headquarters."

THIRTY-TWO

"The chief will be with you in a few minutes," Sergeant Sheppard said, closing the heavy oak door, leaving Nicoletti alone.

The office was on the second floor of an old stone building. Large trees waved their leaves at the double-hung windows and obscured the view of the street. Nicoletti looked around the office.

On the desk was a photo of a buxom blonde who Nicoletti recognized as Jenny Garland. She looked heavier in the photo than she had on Saturday night. In fact, Nicoletti thought, the passing years had been very kind to her.

A second photograph showed Jenny and Peter Garland with their arms around three young boys. They were posed holding a string of cutthroat trout at the rocky edge of a river. Nice family. Jenny and Pete looked younger, happier.

He looked around the room. His attention was drawn to the plaques on the wall behind Garland's desk.

In the center was a diploma from Montana State University. Garland had earned a bachelor of science, and Nicoletti noted it was conferred on the graduate just last year. To the right and left of the diploma were various awards and framed certificates of training. Just right of center was the FBI's National Academy logo. Nicoletti had seen dozens of them prominently displayed behind the desks of high-ranking police managers and chiefs. Garland has a future, Nicoletti thought. The door behind him opened.

"Mr. Nicoletti. Thank you for coming on such short notice," Chief Garland said. "Please, sit down. Sorry to keep you waiting, but we've been busy around here today."

"No problem." Nicoletti eased into a wooden office chair in front of the desk.

"I'm sorry to have brought you here so abruptly, but I wanted to see you before you left the area." Garland sat behind the desk.

"No problem," Nicoletti said again, thinking to himself, *Two times "sorry" means you're not, and two times "no problem" means there is.*

"There are a few things I'd like to discuss with you." Garland shuffled the files on his desk as if he couldn't remember the things to discuss without referencing them. "Can I offer you something to drink? Coffee?"

Nicoletti declined.

"It's not often an investigator of your international reputation finds his way to our part of the world." Garland leaned back in his chair. "I've spoken to some of my men who attended your lecture. They were very impressed with your presentation. They said you expressed several strong opinions regarding police managers, none of them very flattering." He looked at his notes. "'Incompetent buffoons' and 'wasteful political puppets' were two of the least provocative statements you made."

Nicoletti started to offer a mild defense of his comments, but Garland cut him off.

"I've got to tell you, Mr. Nicoletti, I don't have much use for your kind. You fly around the country—or should I say, around the world?—sticking your nose in other people's business, solving crimes you believe the local police are too incompetent to resolve on their own, when the truth is, they could have done very well without your help. Then you give an interview to the local press and ride off into the sunset like the Lone Ranger, leaving the local police looking like fools and dealing with the job of repairing their public image."

Nicoletti did not like the tone of Garland's accusations and responded with a hint of hostility. "I never involve myself in any investigation without an invitation from the local authorities. Their public information officers orchestrate the press coverage. Sometimes they mention my contributions, sometimes they don't. I have no interest in public relations."

"You know, it's not easy for us locals to compete with your image, Mr. Nicoletti. You drink fancy European wine, and use your charm and wit to sweep our women off their feet, maybe make them a little less content with the men in their community, the real men who work hard every day to do their job and live what I suppose you would consider a dull, simple life.

"These are the men you mock with your arrogance. I am the man you joke about in your lectures, and when you leave—flying off to Washington or London or wherever—I am the man left behind to continue the daily work of this city. Only thing is, after you're done, I am diminished in the eyes of my men and all the others who have been exposed to your bullshit international perspective." Garland paused to compose himself.

Nicoletti didn't offer any apologies.

"I've done some checking on you, Nicoletti. I just spoke to a trusted friend at the FBI Academy in Quantico. He told me a great deal about you." Garland shuffled the papers again. "One thing I found very interesting is a story concerning the murder several years ago of Robert McDermott, a DEA agent. I believe you were once partners. Wasn't he your best friend?" Garland dropped his aggression and adopted the air of a tenured university professor. "You were a suspect in that case, weren't you?"

THIRTY-THREE

Nicoletti took a controlled breath before responding to Garland's taunting. "I don't see the necessity to review—"

"I'm sure you don't," Garland said. "But my source said that the only reason you were not more fully implicated in McDermott's murder was because the informant in the case unexpectedly withdrew his accusations against you. Then, before the ink was dry on the retraction, the informant was gunned down by persons unknown." Garland looked hard at Nicoletti. "Shortly after that, you left the country and flew to London for a vacation. Is my information accurate?"

"Those are some of the facts." Nicoletti tried to remain calm. "But if your 'trusted friend' is FBI Agent Derek Reed, he's a petty bureaucrat who bumbled his way through that investigation and squandered any chance of catching the murderers." Nicoletti could feel his blood pressure reaching uncharted territory.

"All these years and the murder of your best friend is still unsolved. How does that make you feel? What is it like for you, the great investigator, knowing the murderer is free to walk the streets? It makes one wonder just how good a detective you really are." Garland switched on the intercom. "Sergeant, come in."

For a moment, Nicoletti considered bashing Garland's skull with the heavy glass ashtray sitting at the corner of the desk. Two men entered the room and approached Nicoletti from the left.

"Mr. Nicoletti, this is Detective Mike Reichert, and you've already met Sergeant Sheppard."

Nicoletti nodded at the two men, who were carrying cardboard boxes. Neither man made any effort to shake Nicoletti's hand. They placed the boxes on the desk next to the ashtray.

Garland was now the master of ceremonies. He moved a file to the center of his desk. "There was a woman murdered last night. Her body was found down by the river near the Harrison Street Bridge." Garland opened the file. "Know the area?"

"I don't think so." The question took Nicoletti off guard. He leaned forward, trying to concentrate. He was a little confused. After all of Garland's insulting remarks and accusations, Nicoletti couldn't believe the man was about to ask him to assist on a murder case. He focused on the question, trying to be helpful. "Wait. Yes, I know it. It crosses the river just this side of the Chez Margot. I crossed it several times the other day."

"Precisely." Garland placed his elbows on the desk. "How did you like the food at Chez Margot?"

Nicoletti felt uneasy. The quick shift in Garland's tone and subject matter was unexpected. There was a leap in logical progression. Garland should have asked if he had eaten there before asking for an evaluation of the cuisine. Nicoletti recognized the technique—it was an interrogator's trick designed to convey knowledge of a suspect's activities. Nicoletti did not like having tricks played on him. He did not like feeling like a suspect. "What does that have to do with the murder?"

"Maybe nothing, but I thought you might have seen the victim at the restaurant. She ate there last night, a few hours before she was killed."

Nicoletti's brain began to churn visual images—the chef, his wife, a middle-aged couple celebrating their anniversary, the two young women seated at the rear table.

"The victim's name is Marie-Justine Cantrell," Garland said flatly. "You met her on Saturday, I believe."

Nicoletti did not process Garland's statement. He was too busy searching the restaurant for female faces, desperately trying not to see Justine sitting across the table from him, trying not to see her smile as he cataloged the list of potential victims.

"Here is a picture of her. Do you remember seeing her the night you were there?" Garland pushed a photograph from the file across the desk. He rested his hands on his chin and waited.

The photograph was of a beautiful woman sitting on a patio. Behind her was a set of French doors painted white with yellow accents. The woman's striking facial features were framed by cascading chestnut hair that, even in the photograph, caught the sun with shining red highlights. She wore a light blue dress that clung sensually to her sculpted body. Her tan legs were crossed in a playful manner that accentuated their musculature. She was wearing white espadrille shoes. Nicoletti wanted to lay next to her in the sunlight.

THIRTY-FOUR

"Let me outline the case for you as we understand it so far. Maybe a famous detective like you will be able to help us solve this grotesque crime." Garland stood up and began pacing behind his desk. "The murder occurred either late last night or early this morning, but I think we should begin with the victim's activities on Saturday morning.

"According to a friend, the victim had gotten up at six, gone for a three-mile run, showered, and had a cup of tea and a brioche. You're probably more familiar with brioche than we are, Mr. Nicoletti." Pleased with his remark, Garland grinned at the other man.

"The victim then called her father in New York. She placed an eight o'clock call to a friend that lasted approximately ten minutes. Then she dropped her car off at a local garage for servicing before meeting a friend at a café on Arthur Avenue at ten o'clock." Garland paused as if to ensure he had Nicoletti's full attention.

"At the café, a witness described a man sitting alone at an outside table near the bicycle rack. The witness said that she observed the man staring at Marie-Justine as if in a trance. This went on for quite a while, apparently. After the man left the restaurant, the victim's friend brought the man's behavior to the victim's attention. Marie-Justine said that she was aware of the man and had the feeling she had known him from somewhere in her past. She even confessed to her friend that she wanted to go over to the man's table and talk to him and would have, if he had not departed so abruptly." Garland turned from the window to Nicoletti. "Pretty weird, don't you think? But you know what is even more interesting? The description we got of the guy matches your description to a T."

"I was at the café. I remember seeing her, and I'm sure I was staring at her. But I did not know her. I had never seen her before then," Nicoletti said. He kept to himself the fact that he also had felt as if he knew Marie-Justine, and it took all the willpower he had not to go to her table.

"Well, that would be that if we didn't have another witness who, a few hours later, saw a man, again matching your description, peeking at the victim through the shrubbery in front of her home."

Garland held up his hand to stop Nicoletti's attempt to interrupt.

"And then later that evening, there are several witnesses, including me, who place the victim in a long conversation with you at Dean Hawkins' home. We also have information that you spent the following day with the victim, and last night she had dinner at the Chez Margot restaurant with a man matching your description. All the witnesses at Chez Margot described their conversation as very friendly. Some thought the man was Marie-Justine's lover." Garland turned his gaze to the men standing behind Nicoletti. "That was the word some of them used, right, Detective Reichert?"

"Right, Chief. 'Lovers' was quoted in two of the witness statements," Reichert said on cue. "The statements also provided a description of the man, which matches pretty close to Mr. Nicoletti here, and the restaurant owners were introduced to him by name. So there is no doubt—."

"Thank you, Detective." Garland moved the boxes closer to his side of the desk. "Now we have these items." He held up a series of clear plastic evidence bags. "A champagne bottle and two glasses. We've lifted several sets of latent prints off these, some of which I would be willing to wager are going to be remarkably close to yours, Nicoletti.

"We also found this in the vicinity of what we believe to be the location of the initial struggle between the victim and her killer." He lifted a bag containing a silver-and-gold pen. "The inscription says 'G/S J. Nicoletti,' a name that is remarkably similar to yours." Garland was enjoying the rhythmic sound of his performance.

"Then we have this green down vest that was found near the body. There is a smear and several drops of dried blood on it, possibly containing DNA similar to yours." He placed the items back in the boxes.

"We also pulled your hotel's phone number off the victim's cell phone, which was found in her car parked near the bridge." Garland stopped the performance and nodded toward Reichert.

"We would like you to sign this Consent to Search form," Reichert said, handing the paper to Nicoletti, "giving us permission to search your hotel room for any evidence that we believe may be associated with this crime."

Nicoletti took a pen from the chief's desk, signed the form, and handed it back to Reichert without saying a word.

"We would also appreciate it if you would voluntarily provide us with your fingerprints and a DNA sample," Reichert said.

Nicoletti turned in his seat to face the detective and nodded his head. He stood and looked at Garland. "I'm not the man you're looking for. While you waste your time with me, the real killer is getting away." Nicoletti struggled to control the quiver in his voice.

"We are not taking you into custody at this time," Garland said. "Although, to tell you the truth, I'm tempted. But FBI Agent Pandori has advised me against it, out of respect for your reputation, I suppose. So, as a courtesy to him, you are free to go, but not too far. I'll need you for a lineup as soon as the witnesses are assembled, probably tomorrow. When the fingerprint comparisons are complete, Detective Reichert will be in touch."

THIRTY-FIVE

Detective Reichert escorted Nicoletti down a narrow hallway at the back of the courthouse. He pushed the panic bar on a steel door and threw it open. The bright sunlight temporarily blinded Nicoletti and he hesitated. Reichert grabbed him by the bicep and pushed him through the door into the parking lot.

Lenny Pandori was leaning on the side of his Jeep, chewing on the remains of a cigar. He opened the passenger door for Nicoletti. Neither man spoke. Pandori closed the door and walked over to Reichert, who handed him a large envelope. They exchanged a few words that Nicoletti could not hear. Then Pandori got in the Jeep, started the engine, and drove slowly out of the parking lot and down a back street.

"You want to go get a drink, or go to my place, or—"

"You should have called me," Nicoletti said.

"I did call you. I called the hotel and your cell. I left you messages. I've been sitting in my office for the last two hours, waiting for you to call me back."

"The phones at the hotel aren't working and I shut my cell phone off. I got tired of the guys at the law firm calling me every fifteen minutes."

"Well, turn the fucking thing on. You may need to talk to those lawyers before this is over."

"That's bullshit. This is ridiculous." Nicoletti lit a cigarette and rolled the window down.

"You don't get it, do you?" Pandori pulled the shredded wet end of the cigar from his mouth. "Garland is dead serious. A woman has been murdered, and he's going to lock someone up for it, even if it's you."

"He's not dumb enough to try and pin this on me. He could never make it stick."

"He's not interested in convicting you. He needs an arrest. I told you he's going to run for sheriff. His campaign starts in a few months. He won't want this killing unsolved so it can be used against him by his opponent." Pandori pulled a wet strand of tobacco off his bottom lip and threw it out the window. "And it's not just Garland. The district attorney, the state attorney general, hell, even the governor—they're all tied together. If any one of them falls and stumbles between now and next November, they may all take a hit."

"Drop me off at the hotel."

"Are you listening to me? So they gather enough evidence for an indictment. You have no alibi, am I right?"

Nicoletti did not answer.

"So you're arrested, maybe in the spring. Your lawyer waives any speedy trial issues in hopes they'll catch the real killer. They'll have you awaiting trial all summer and through the fall, hoping the election goes off without a hitch. Even if they drop the case against you after the election, they've got what they wanted and you're fucked."

"What's the story on Detective Reichert?" Nicoletti asked.

"Mike's a good guy, good detective. Came here from the Baltimore PD about two years ago."

"What's his take on this?"

"He's not saying. I don't think he's buying the idea that you were involved." Pandori spit a piece of tobacco out the window. "Reichert called me to take a look at the crime scene. He also called me to pick you up at the back door."

"And Garland?"

"Put yourself in his shoes. Look at the evidence he's got. Think about his situation. Nico, I can't make this any clearer…it's not about who killed Marie-Justine; right now, it's all about politics. By tomorrow morning, this will be in every newspaper in the state. If the cops don't bring it to a quick resolution, every woman within three hundred miles will think she sees the killer hiding in her vegetable garden.

The Jeep pulled up in front of the hotel lobby. Nicoletti went inside and got his messages—three from the law firm, one from Pandori. He returned to the car and stopped at the driver's window.

"I got your message." Nicoletti put the message slips in his pocket. "They tell me the phones are working now."

"Hey, want to get some dinner?" Pandori asked.

"No. I just need some time to think." Nicoletti started to walk away.

"Want to take a look at these crime scene photos?" Pandori held up the envelope he had gotten from Reichert.

Nicoletti shook his head. "No."

"Hey, Nico, if you think you need to take a couple of hours to sort things out, that's up to you. But you better pull your head out of your ass, and sooner is better than later." Pandori turned the Jeep toward the street. "And turn on your damn cell phone."

·   ·   ·

Charles Durbin watched from across the street as Nicoletti walked up the stairs to his room.

"Well, Mr. Nicoletti," Durbin said, "was the big-time investigator from Washington, DC, able to help the little Missoula police department? I think not."

THIRTY-SIX

Nicoletti hung up his jacket, then took the cell phone from his briefcase and turned it on. He had four messages. He listened to the beginning of each one before deleting it without allowing it to finish. As he started to place the phone back in the briefcase, it rang. The caller ID showed the call was from his office.

"Nico, where the hell have you been? I've been trying to reach you all day." The caller, Joan Krieger, was on speakerphone and sounded pissed.

"I've had some trouble with the phones here."

"The Humboldt case starts next week, in case you have forgotten." Nicoletti imagined her with her hands on her hips, walking back and forth behind her desk. "We need to have another strategy conference. When are you coming back?"

"My flight is for Sunday afternoon," he lied. He was booked on Thursday. "I'll land at Dulles about seven."

"Christ, can't you get back here sooner?" He could hear her tapping a pen on the edge of the desk. "We need to talk this over."

"Joan, we discussed this case before I left. You have the investigative file and the tapes of all my interviews. Unless the defense has come up with a new medical expert, there really isn't much more I can do for you at this point." He was exhausted and wanted to disconnect the call. Hell, she was the lawyer; he was just the investigator.

"I just want to be sure we've covered all the bases. I don't want to leave that butcher of a doctor and his slob lawyer any room to wriggle out of this." Nicoletti knew Joan Krieger's routine. She would now change her tactics by softening her voice and playing to Nicoletti's sympathy for their client. He decided to save her the trouble of the charade.

"I'll see what I can do about rebooking on an earlier flight," he said, even though he had no intention of doing so.

"Joe, you're the best. Thanks. Call me as soon as you land."

As soon as Nicoletti dropped the cell phone into the open briefcase, the hotel phone rang. Nicoletti was not going to answer it. The ringing stopped for a moment, then it started again. He picked up the receiver.

"Mr. Nicoletti, this is Jason Kimba."

"Yes, Doctor, what can I do for you?"

"I just heard the news on the radio; they announced it was Marie-Justine." The doctor sounded desperate. "I thought we should meet as soon as possible."

"Won't tomorrow be soon enough?" Nicoletti sat on the edge of the bed.

"I do not think it's wise to delay."

"Doctor, I must tell you, they have identified me as their prime suspect."

"They are so misguided." Kimba exhaled forcefully. "All the more reason to meet at once. I am still at the university. It's just past six. I have a meeting with one of my graduate assistants, but that won't take long. I'll meet you at my home. How does seven fifteen sound?"

Nicoletti gave in. "Seven thirty sounds better."

"Seven thirty it is. All I have is scotch and a bit of wine."

"Scotch is good." Nicoletti hung up. Something in Dr. Kimba's tone set Nicoletti slightly on edge. *I don't think it is wise to delay.* He picked up the cell phone and attached it to his belt.

THIRTY-SEVEN

Dr. Jason Kimba set two cut crystal glasses next to the ice bucket and water pitcher on the desk in his library office. From an oak cabinet he took the file labeled CHARLES DURBIN. He had stopped assigning numbers to his patients' files when he no longer had a staff to protect them from.

He placed the file in the center of the desk, next to his appointment book, on the green blotter with brown leather trim. He turned on the desk lamp and looked around the room, forcing his eyes past the painting of the Broadmoor fountain. Helen's work had always brought him so much joy. Now, her painting, hanging above the mantel, made him fearful. Durbin had robbed him of a simple pleasure with a needless lie.

The wind rattled the wood-framed windows. Dr. Kimba heard the scratching of branches against the wooden clapboard siding. From the center drawer of the desk, he took his derringer and lowered it into the right pocket of his tweed jacket.

He dropped three ice cubes into one of the heavy crystal glasses and covered them with scotch and a splash of water. He thought about lighting a fire. He looked at his watch. 7:15. He would wait until Nicoletti arrived and let him decide if a fire was needed.

Sipping the scotch, he felt a chill and headed to his bedroom to put on a sweater. He crossed the wooden parquet floor in the dining room and stopped at the front door. He unlocked it and flipped the switch for the porch light. The light did not come on.

"That's odd," he said aloud, peering through the sheer curtain covering the door's elongated center window. "I just replaced that light." He set the glass on a small table next to the door.

He stepped onto the porch and stretched toward the overhead fixture. With his fingertips, he was able to rotate the bulb a quarter turn. It illuminated. He closed the door and picked up his glass. Leaving the light from the porch behind, he climbed the wooden staircase toward the darkness of the second floor.

He chose the burgundy sweater Helen had given him for Christmas the year the university had granted him tenure. He pulled on the sports coat, felt the weight of the derringer in the pocket, took a sip of scotch, and turned off the bedroom light.

As he stepped into the darkness of the second floor hallway, he heard something rustle behind him. He paused. Listened. Only the wind. He moved toward the staircase.

"Dr. Kimba." A voice came from the darkness.

His back tingled. Without warning, a gloved hand took the crystal glass and threw it down the stairs. Dr. Kimba jammed his right hand into the coat pocket, but it was too late. He was in the air, being hurled toward the stairs. He crashed against the wooden stairs, tumbling, losing his sense of up and down. His head thudded against the plaster wall, the wooden stair treads, the wall again.

His left cheek burned. It was pressed against the parquet floor and he could not lift his head. Dr. Kimba saw the light from the porch refracted by broken glass and puddles of liquid next to his face. He heard footsteps coming down the stairs. He struggled to pull the derringer from his pocket, but his arm and hand would not obey him.

The footsteps stopped and the toe of a heavy boot appeared near his right shoulder. "You failed, Doctor. I came to you for help, and what did I get?" The boot pressed down hard against his right elbow. "I know what you were planning to do. You were going to tell the police about your peculiar patient."

"Charles, please," Kimba said. He heard breathing close to the back of his head.

"You cannot help the police. They must struggle on their own." The voice was close to his ear. "You know I lied to you. Everything was a lie."

Dr. Kimba felt the gloved hands slide along his cheekbones. Then the gloves lifted his head and pulled it back. The boot pressed into the center of his back. He saw the light through the curtain and remembered the porch light at Marie-Justine's cottage. He thought of Helen handing him the burgundy sweater on Christmas morning.

Charles Durbin twisted the doctor's head with a quick jerking motion. There was a muffled snap. Then he dropped the head onto the wooden floor.

A car engine rattled into the driveway. Durbin peered through the sheer curtain on the front door and saw Nicoletti.

*   *   *

The taxi backed out of the drive as Nicoletti walked to the front door and rang the bell. He waited a minute and rang again. He knocked on the door. The porch light reflecting off the sheer curtain that covered the glass in the door kept him from seeing inside. He stepped to the left of the door and peered through the window. There was no movement inside. He could see the silhouette of the dining room table and chairs. There was a light on in a back room. He walked back to the door, knocked again, then grasped the curved door handle and depressed the latch. The door opened.

He entered partway. "Dr. Kimba? It's Joe Nicoletti." The house was quiet.

He stepped fully into the entry. Through the open doorway, the porch light cast a rectangle of illumination on the wooden floor—Nicoletti stood at one end of the rectangle; at the other end was the body of Dr. Kimba. Spattered liquid and broken glass reflected the light.

Nicoletti stepped around the edge of the door and pushed it shut. He bent down next to the body. Dr. Kimba's right eye was open. He touched it, but there was no reaction.

He stood up and stepped away from the body. He did not move; he did not breathe. He listened. He strained to hear above the sound of his blood rushing through his body. He looked up the stairs to the darkened hallway on the second floor before moving toward the light in the office.

His cell phone rang. It was Lenny Pandori.

"Hold on." Nicoletti sensed someone was at the back of the house. He held his breath and listened, but there was no sound and no one there.

"I'm at Dr. Kimba's. There's been an accident. Looks like he might have fallen down the stairs.... Yeah, he's hurt—fatally.... I'm sure.... No, I haven't called anyone. I just got here. You call the cops.... Yeah, I'll be right here.... Hold on." Nicoletti walked back to the front door and stepped onto the porch. He found the brass numbers to the left of the door. "It's 2735 on Princeton Avenue. Hey, you'd better call Reichert and Garland. I don't want to have to explain this twice."

THIRTY-EIGHT

Nicoletti leaned back in the leather chair and studied Helen Kimba's painting of the fountain and garden. He had explained three times how he had come to be at Dr. Kimba's home; first he explained it to Detective Reichert and Lenny Pandori, who had arrived simultaneously, then twice more to Chief Garland.

"I just wonder," Garland said, sitting behind Dr. Kimba's desk, "if the doctor had information that might have been useful to the police, why would he call you?" Garland opened his notebook and set it in the middle of the green blotter.

"I have no idea. Maybe he was unsure of what he had and wanted a second opinion before calling you."

"So he told you he was going to call us?"

"No, he never said."

"And he never mentioned the patient's name?"

"I told you twice, no." Nicoletti's reply was quiet. "Look, I've told you all I know. All you have to do is check his files." He pointed to the oak cabinet. "Somewhere in there is a file on a thirty-year-old male with an alcoholic mother. He's a Peeping Tom who had kinky sex with an older woman when he was twelve. How many nut-jobs can there be who match that description?"

"Don't tell me what I need to do." Garland raised his voice, then he regained his composure. "I'll tell you what I think…A woman was murdered. You talked to Dr. Kimba, and something you said made him suspect that you were the killer. You realized that you screwed up, and you came here tonight to put a permanent end to his suspicion and make sure he couldn't tell the police."

"That's the first intelligent thing I've heard you say since I met you," Nicoletti said.

"Is that a confession?"

"Let's drop the bullshit, Garland. If you really thought I was the killer, you'd have locked me up this afternoon."

"I may lock you up tonight, if you give me half a reason."

"If Dr. Kimba's fall was not an accident, then you're right, there probably is a connection to Marie-Justine's murder and probably for the very reason you said: someone wanted to shut him up before he disclosed whatever he knew about the killer."

"If it was not an accident, if there is a mysterious patient, and if that patient can be tied to Marie-Justine, then maybe we've got something. If not, I've still got you."

"Don't be an ass." Nicoletti leaned on the desk. "There's another thing you need to consider. Unless I'm wrong, Reichert is the only detective you've got with experience. The others are just following his lead or mimicking what they've seen in the movies. If Reichert is working the two stabbings and Dr. Kimba's death, he'll never be able to focus on Marie-Justine's murder. Every minute that goes by, her killer is getting further away, or worse, is getting closer to his next kill."

Lenny Pandori and Detective Reichert walked into the study.

"What have we got?" Garland asked.

"Looks like an accident, but maybe not," Reichert said. "There's some glass embedded in the doctor's left cheek. It's possible the ME can tell if he was still alive when he hit the bottom of the stairs and landed on the broken glass." Reichert looked at his notepad. "I've got photos of the scene, for what it's worth. But Nicoletti, two paramedics, and two patrol officers danced through it before I got here, and you and Deputy Chief McKay walked through the area before I took the pictures. The paramedics moved the body. The officers did a sweep of the house when they arrived—went in every room, every closet, and the basement. So if there was any evidence of value, it's probably been disturbed or destroyed. Where we go from here is anybody's guess."

Chief Garland made notes in his book. Then he pointed his pen at Reichert. "I want the neighbors interviewed tonight. It's only nine o'clock. Have McKay call in additional officers and let's get this started. You know the drill." He looked at Nicoletti, then turned back to Reichert. "Mike, have the officers specifically ask if anyone remembers seeing a male in his thirties visiting the doctor yesterday."

"What time?" Reichert asked.

Garland looked to Nicoletti, who shrugged his shoulders.

"Any time. If they get a description, run it by the other neighbors to see if the subject was a regular visitor." Garland made another entry in his notebook. He glanced at Nicoletti before continuing, "And tell McKay I want to see him. He's going to run the Kimba inquiry. I'll tell him to keep you fully briefed. And give the stabbings to one of your guys. I want you on the Cantrell murder full-time, starting now."

Reichert left the room and Garland looked at Pandori.

"Lenny, what the hell are you doing here anyway? Is accidental death now part of the FBI's jurisdiction?"

"Nico told me to come." Pandori looked at Nicoletti.

Garland stood up and closed his notebook. He crossed the room and opened the back door. "I want the two of you out of here. Pandori, stop by my office tomorrow at nine and don't bring your friend."

Nicoletti pulled the door of Pandori's Jeep closed. He rolled down the window and lit a cigarette. "I'd like to see the photographs you got from Reichert this afternoon."

"It's about time you pulled your head out of your ass."

THIRTY-NINE

Marie-Justine sat on the edge of the bed smiling. She extended her left arm and coaxed Nicoletti close to her. Her skin was supple and fragrant with perfume. He eased back onto the pillow and guided her smoothly to his lips. She rested upon him gently, like a mist slowly enveloping the green hillsides of spring. Her chestnut hair flowed over his face and encased him in its silken beauty. He felt her warm hands moving along his torso, rubbing his shoulder, and coming to rest along the sides of his neck. She began to squeeze him slowly.

He could feel the pressure of her hands against his carotid arteries increase. He felt thirst. He needed air. Pressure began to build behind his eyes. He tried to push her away, but his arms were lifeless at his sides. The hands tightened their grip, and her arms extended as she forced the weight of her body forward.

He struggled to see her face shrouded in her hair. He began to panic. Then he realized it was not her hair but a hood, a gray hood, concealing the face in darkness. He arched his back and twisted to the right in an attempt to throw the attacker from a position of dominance.

He struggled, trying to force his hands to move quickly. They floated without power as if moving through a heavy, viscous liquid.

He pushed his left hand to his throat and grabbed the sinewy forearm protruding from the gray sleeve. It was a man's arm, muscle and tendons, strong and defined. He clenched his right fist, now suddenly alive, and drove it into the center of the massive gray parka.

Lunging upward, Nicoletti screamed aloud, "Where is she? What have you done with her?"

The room was silent and dark. Nicoletti was upright in the bed, the covers strewn. He was damp with perspiration and shivered in the cold. The clock radio read 5:00 A.M.

He tried to control his breathing. Was he going insane? He had lost himself in a woman he hardly knew. She occupied his waking moments, and now, for the second time, she dominated his sleep. This time, she had brought with her a killer—a presence so real, Nicoletti could still feel the iron hands upon his throat. Insane or not, he was determined to avenge her.

FORTY

At nine o'clock the next morning, the hotel phone rang. Nicoletti wiped the remaining shaving cream from his chin and took a long sip from his third cup of coffee before picking up the receiver.

"Nico, it's me," his son-in-law, Thomas Marley, said. "I thought I'd better give you a heads up. I got a call last night from a *Denver Post* reporter named Anne Bertone. Apparently, she's up there in Missoula. Know her?"

"I've met her," Nicoletti said.

"Well, somehow she knows you. I guess there was a woman murdered there the other day and she wanted to know a little about your background, see if you were the right guy to help out the local police on their investigation."

"Why would she call you?" Nicoletti asked.

"She covered a case we did last year—outlaw biker gang moving heroin and weapons here in Denver. She did a good job; she gave a balanced report, which came out very favorable to our efforts. She was tough, smart, and not too hard on the eyes. You know what I mean?"

"What did you tell her?"

"I told her if I was murdered, I would want you hunting the killer. So I guess she'll be in touch. Hey, about that ranch we were talking about…"

"I'll get back to you on that." Nicoletti cut him short. "Someone is knocking on my door."

Anne Bertone was dressed in black. Her short, raven hair was combed back from her face and she wore no makeup. Her manner was crisp with only a hint of courtesy. "Hi, Joe. Anne Bertone. Remember me? I'm Marie-Justine's friend. We met Saturday night." She extended her right hand and shook his firmly. "I was wondering if we could talk."

"Sure, come in."

"Not now, I don't have time. I will be spending the morning with M-J's father and her ex-husband. Can we talk tomorrow after I take her father to the airport?"

"Yes, certainly. Can we plan on about twelve thirty, or anytime after that?" Nicoletti realized he was still shaking her hand and let it go.

"Yes. I'll call you tomorrow after twelve thirty."

"What is this about? I—"

"Tomorrow," she said, walking away. "That's if you're not arrested by then."

FORTY-ONE

Nicoletti spent the rest of the morning at the university as a member of a conference panel discussion. The topic was "Major Case Management" and it focused on multiple jurisdictional investigations. His mood was too aggressive for the forum.

Every question asked by the audience and every answer given by the panel members made him more anxious. He had no patience for any of them. They were talking in the abstract and he was only thinking of reality—the reality of Marie-Justine's murder in Missoula.

His review of the crime scene photos and Pandori's description of the collected evidence had convinced him beyond all doubt that Justine had been the victim of a serial killer, an experienced and mature killer.

The lack of defensive wounds and bruising gave testimony to the swiftness of the initial attack. He was not clumsy, not a youngster out for a thrill.

There had to be planning. The killer's use of a ligature, the combing of the hair, the application of makeup, and the red velvet choker all added up to the fulfillment of a well-defined fantasy—a fantasy that was developed over several years of trial and error.

Maybe he was still developing the fantasy. The next victim would tell the tale.

In any event, it was not the sort of violent attack perpetrated by a crazed madman. This killing required a level of control. He was an organized killer. All the items had to be brought to the scene, used in a deliberate manner, and removed, along with a trophy: her underwear.

At this point, there was no way to tell how long the killer had been focusing on her, but Nicoletti was sure the attack was not random. Pandori had agreed. Now he was impatient to meet with Reichert and find out what was being done to find the killer before he struck again.

When the session ended, he took a cab to his hotel. A message was waiting for him. Following the directions in the message, he found himself seated across from an elderly gentleman in a hotel room three doors down the hall from his own.

The elderly man had introduced himself as Dr. Louis Junot, Marie-Justine's father. The man's cane, which had a grapevine carved into the curve of the silver handle, leaned against the wall near the door. Dr. Junot handed Nicoletti a glass of wine.

"Mr. Nicoletti, I am a man of science. I deal in facts, rarely in circumstance. This morning, Police Chief Garland filled my head with his facts, trying to assure me he had the solution to my daughter's murder well within his grasp. I must tell you, I do not believe that to be the case."

He sipped from his glass and lit a cigarette.

"I read a letter today written by my daughter the night she died. She talks of you in a way that prevents me from considering you as anything but her friend, or perhaps more precisely, her lover."

"A letter?" Nicoletti said. "May I see it?" His first reaction should have been to obtain a possible piece of evidence for review, but he was overcome with the thought of a letter written in her hand. He wanted it. He wanted to see her words, to hold them close to his chest as he would never to be able to hold Justine again. He looked at her father and saw a man not as old as he appeared, a man controlling his grief in order to continue his words.

"I do not have it. The police are retaining it as part of their evidence. But it is because of this letter that I asked you to meet with me."

He set his wine glass on the small table between them.

"I want you to know more about Marie-Justine. She was a special person, not just to me, but to everyone she ever met. From birth, she seemed enlightened with a special gift of life and the ability to perceive the spiritual forces that move through the destiny of men.

"The day she was born, her mother, Marie, died from complications the attending physician was powerless to stop. Her maternal grandmother, Justine, had passed away several years before, and so my only child was named Marie-Justine in their memory."

For the better part of an hour, and the better part of the bottle of wine, Dr. Junot described memory upon memory. She was born near Toulon on the southern coast of France. He told of the first time she ever saw snow. It was at the house of her grandfather, in the mountains of the Luberon. She was barely three. When she had awoken that snowy morning, she rushed outside and danced among the crystalline flakes swirling in the vineyard until her grand-père, Joseph, gathered her up in a blanket and deposited her on the wooden kitchen floor. She took her shoes and his boots and placed them in front of the kitchen fireplace just as her grandmother, Justine, had done for all the winters of her marriage to Joseph.

Dr. Junot recalled how the grandfather had watched her with tears in her eyes. Then she turned to him, smiling, and said, "Don't cry, *mon trésor.*"

"My treasure, you see. That was what her grandmother had always called her grandfather in their private moments. But Marie-Justine could not have known that. And to place the frozen boots before the fire… A child of the Mediterranean could not possibly have that knowledge at her age.

"That was the beginning. From that moment on, Joseph called her Justine and they shared a connection—a spiritual communion of some sort. I am sorry to say that I was not a part of their telepathic connection. I never understood it, but I respected it." He divided the last of the wine between them.

"She asked me to call her Justine," Nicoletti said.

"I suppose to her it made perfect sense. Like her grand-père, your name was Joseph, so she decided to be your Justine."

The doctor continued relaying memories of his child, including her school days and her time at university where she blossomed into a beautiful woman.

"That is where she met her best friend, Anne Bertone." He reminisced about the holidays they would take together—he, Marie-Justine, and Anne—reflecting how the girls were more like sisters than friends.

"Anne shares that gift, you know—the knowing of people's souls and things to come. I do not believe it is as strong in Anne, but it is there nonetheless. At least it is there according to Grand-père Joseph. And I suppose he should know. Except for the Great War, he has spent a lifetime in the mountains, talking with the grapevines, the streams, the wind, and the forest. Oh yes, and his dogs, the Great Pyrenees—massive white, furry beasts that care only for him, Marie-Justine, and Anne. The rest of the world they either attack or ignore."

Nicoletti sensed that Dr. Junot was beginning to recede into a slightly distant place—grief, fatigue, memories. Maybe all of them, he could not tell. But knew it was time for him to leave the man alone with his thoughts. As he opened the door, the doctor called to him.

"Tomorrow I will leave to take my daughter back to her grand-père's vineyard to join her mother and grand-mère. When that is done, I will return to Geneva. But you, Mr. Nicoletti, you must remain. To help the police. To punish her killer. You are the one."

He walked to the door and took Nicoletti's hand.

"When I called Grand-père Joseph last night to tell him of the terrible news, he said he already knew. That Marie-Justine had visited him in a dream and told him she was leaving."

Nicoletti was about to tell the doctor that his daughter had also visited him in dreams, but decided against it.

"Grand-père Joseph also told me that when I drink wine with her guardian—and I assure you, Mr. Nicoletti, this is the only wine I have tasted on this journey—I am to tell him not to blame himself, that there was not enough time. Those were his words, Mr. Nicoletti. So do not blame yourself."

FORTY-TWO

"Anything else you want to add?" Detective Reichert asked Nicoletti.

"No, that's everything I can remember." Nicoletti signed the last page of his statement.

"I'll send this to Deputy Chief McKay's office," Reichert said.

"Where is McKay? I thought he was handling the inquiry into Dr. Kimba's death?"

"He's with the chief. They are dealing with the reporters, who are crawling all over the building." Reichert tossed the statement in his out-box.

"Now, concerning your statement regarding Mrs. Cantrell"…Reichert took several handwritten pages from a file folder. "Is there any additional information you can add to this?"

"No, nothing else." Nicoletti hesitated. He had hoped Pandori would be present when he talked to Reichert. "How is the investigation going? Where are we now?"

"We? There is no 'we.' You're still a suspect—a co-operative one, but a suspect nonetheless— and I'm the detective who is not at liberty to discuss the case with you."

"I just thought I might—"

"I'll have your statement typed up and you can sign the final draft tomorrow." Reichert slid the papers back into the file. "Stop by in the morning."

Nicoletti stopped at the door, sensing there was something more Reichert wanted to say. "Is there something else?" Nicoletti asked.

"Nothing that can't wait until tomorrow." Reichert opened a thick manila envelope, reached into it, and pulled out a fistful of small pieces of paper that he waved at Nicoletti. "See you about nine."

In the lobby of the police station, Nicoletti passed a group of reporters. A woman standing next to a cameraman was speaking to the desk officer.

"We are running out of time. How much longer will it be before Chief Garland will be available?"

"He's in a conference. I'll announce you as soon as I am notified that he is free." The officer looked at Nicoletti, who had stopped at the end of the receptionist's window.

"Could I have a piece of paper and a pencil, please?" he said, pushing past the female reporter. Angling the paper on the narrow counter, he wrote:

Chief: My advice would be not to talk directly to the press. Let McKay or someone lower in rank do the talking. Not the best political campaign advice, but better for the investigation. Nicoletti

He folded the paper and handed it to the desk officer. "Give this to the chief before his meeting with McKay is over." He nodded at the reporter as he walked out the door.

The officer left her desk with Nicoletti's note in hand and went to the chief's office. McKay opened the door, received the note, and handed it to Garland.

"What's that?" McKay asked.

"Nothing." Garland read the note, folded it, and placed it under the blotter on his desk. "Let's hear the fax from the LAPD."

"It's a copy of an article from this morning's *Los Angeles Times*. The headline reads:

𝕷𝖔𝖘 𝕬𝖓𝖌𝖊𝖑𝖊𝖘 𝕿𝖎

UCLA PROFESSOR MURDERED IN MONTANA

MISSOULA, Mont.—The body of former UCLA professor Marie-Justine Cantrell was found in a wooded area of Missoula, Montana, yesterday morning, the apparent victim of a homicide.

Professor Cantrell, the estranged wife of noted Los Angeles heart surgeon Dr. Richard Cantrell, had moved to Missoula six months ago to take a position at the University of Montana.

Missoula Police Chief Peter Garland could not be reached for comment, but Undersheriff Doug Martin, a spokesperson for the local sheriff's office, stated that Professor Cantrell's body had been discovered early Monday morning by two school children. Martin said that significant evidence had been discovered at the crime scene and at the victim's home. The spokesperson added that a suspect had already been identified and that the sheriff's department was assisting the police with the investigation.

Professor Cantrell, described by friends as beautiful and brilliant, had been a fixture in the LA social scene until her separation from her husband two years ago. Gene Gallatin, chairperson of the LA Committee for the Arts, said—

"That's enough," Garland said.

"They go on to say that the husband is traveling to Montana to assist the police." McKay looked up.

"Enough. Leave it. I'll read it later." Garland took the folded note from under the blotter and read it again. "That fucking Doug Martin can't keep his goddamn name out of the papers or his yap shut." He set the note on his desk and sat down to write. "I'm going to write out a statement I want you to read to the press."

"Don't you think it's better if they hear it from you?" McKay said. "I mean, it would do you good to be in front of the cameras, with the election and all."

"Read this to them"—Garland kept writing—"and don't add anything. Tell them this is all we're going to say." He handed the paper to McKay.

"This isn't much. What if they ask why you're not giving the briefing?"

"Tell them I'm involved in the investigation, and from now on, you will be the only spokesman for the department."

"You mean 'spokes*person*.'" McKay took the statement and walked into the hall.

"Straighten your tie. And tuck in that damn shirt."

Garland opened Nicoletti's note and read it again before throwing it in the trash.

FORTY-THREE

Nicoletti walked from the police station to the hotel. He started up the outside staircase to his room, then turned back and headed to the grocery store next door. He walked slowly, thinking of the things Dr. Junot had said: *Tell her guardian not to blame himself.*

Who else was there to blame? How did he become her guardian? Justine had entered his life and suddenly it was his responsibility to protect her? That was absurd. What was he to do? How could he have known she was in danger?

He stopped the questions that tortured his brain. Then he became angry with himself. He should have sensed it. That was his skill, his talent—to feel the presence of impending doom. He had failed. Carried away with an inner peace he had not known for years, he shut off the receptors that had served him so well.

Marie-Justine had given him a glimpse of the way life could be. For a few hours, she had filled his mind and soul with life. She had given him the hope of a world far away from the violence that had dominated his last thirty years. She had taught him that he still had the capacity to love. That Kristen's death was not his death. Now Marie-Justine was dead, and with her gone, he felt himself drifting back into the darkness of anger and revenge.

He was a fool to believe that his life would be changed. To believe treachery and evil would cease to exist just because Marie-Justine had returned him to a place of tranquility and peace was nonsense. What the hell had he been thinking?

Standing in front of the grocery store's meager wine selection, he heard a familiar voice.

"Are you buying a gift for me, Mr. Nicoletti?" Dean Hawkins' wife was standing at the end of the aisle, her arms full of fruit, bottled water, and yogurt.

"No, I was buying a tranquilizer for myself." Nicoletti tried to muster a smile.

"Well, I don't want to keep you. Your friend is waiting."

"Who?" Nicoletti took a bottle of red Bordeaux from the shelf.

"The young man in the gray parka. I saw you walking with him from the hotel as I was parking my car."

"I wasn't walking with anyone," Nicoletti said, placing the bottle in front of the cashier.

"Of course you were. He's the same man you were with yesterday afternoon in front of the art gallery downtown. Now, you can't deny that. I was inside the gallery, looking at some frames. When I came out to say hello, the two of you were gone." She put her groceries on the counter. "He's out in front of the store, waiting for you. I passed him as I came in."

Nicoletti was convinced that the dean's wife had a screw loose. Maybe all she needed was to put on a few pounds to help her synapses fire in sequence.

They carried their purchases out of the store and Mrs. Hawkins scanned the parking area. "I don't see him now," she said. "But I swear he was just here."

"Maybe it was one of Chief Garland's men, keeping an eye on me to make sure I don't leave town."

"Why would Garland be interested in your travel plans?"

Nicoletti avoided the truth. "He's asked me to provide him with a little assistance."

"Oh yes, with those terrible murders." She put her groceries in the trunk of her car. "It must be awful to deal with such matters. And poor Marie-Justine. She was such a lovely person—so intelligent and so beautiful."

"Yes, well, I've got to get going," Nicoletti said, eager to end the conversation.

"And Jason Kimba, how awful." She clearly had no intention of letting him go until she had finished. "Such a terrible accident. You know, I almost fell down those stairs myself a few years ago. Jason was showing my husband and me some of Helen's paintings in the upstairs hall. They were paintings of the Greek islands. We started down the stairs for dinner and I lost my balance. Luckily, Jason caught my arm or I'd have gone tumbling." She jingled her keys and opened her driver's door. "Well, I must hurry along. My better half will be expecting his dinner on the table soon, and I like to get home before it gets too dark."

Nicoletti walked back to the hotel, scanning for the phantom companion the dean's wife imagined.

•   •   •

At the other end of the grocery store parking lot, inside the charcoal-gray Suburban, Charles Durbin took a large hunting knife from the inside pocket of his gray parka. He ran his thumb over the green-and-yellow embroidered ribbon that was sewn onto the brown leather sheath. Then he drew the knife slowly from the sheath. The afternoon sunlight struck the blade, illuminating the military emblem etched into the polished steel. Etched above the emblem was the inscription LT. COL. REGINALD CALLOWAY, U.S. ARMY, 1965–1995. He slid the knife back into the sheath and put it in the console of the truck.

After he watched Nicoletti walk toward the hotel, Durbin drove through the quiet residential streets of the university area. They were the streets where Marie-Justine had lived in her yellow-and-white cottage, where she had tended her garden, where she had sipped her tea in the sun. They were the same quiet streets where Anne Bertone lived in a one-story house with green trim—another house that Durbin knew well.

FORTY-FOUR

By ten o'clock Wednesday morning, Detective Reichert's desk was completely covered with file folders, large manila envelopes, and a series of yellow legal pads with notes and diagrams on each.

Nicoletti signed the typed statements and laid them on the folder marked NICOLETTI. Then Lenny Pandori handed him fifteen pages of a partially filled out Violent Criminal Apprehension Program form. Nicoletti read through it.

"There's really not enough information at this point to make a complete ViCAP entry," Pandori said.

"If you keep it a little more general, you might at least get some links to similar crimes in western states. It might give you something to work with," Nicoletti said. "Later, after the lab work comes back, you can narrow it down to attacks that are more similar."

"Please," Reichert said, "I've got too much information already." He waved his arms across his desk. "It's going to take two months just to get through the leads we've gotten in the last forty-eight hours."

Nicoletti walked to the window and looked out at the police parking lot. In the corner of the lot, inside a chain-link cage, was Marie-Justine's silver Mercedes.

"You can't waste that much time," Nicoletti said. "If the killer is mobile, just passing through, and has acted out in multiple jurisdictions, then maybe he's already moved on. If that's the case, you have time, and believe me, you're going to need plenty of time to get organized and coordinated with other departments." He turned back to Pandori and Reichert. "But if the killer is local and he's started harvesting victims in this area, then you'd better move quickly, or all you're going to have time for is crime scene searches and cataloging evidence. You'll never have time to figure out who did it."

"Look at this mess," Reichert said. "I've got names of her students, friends, guys she dated only once; a partial list of over-the-road truckers who spent Saturday and Sunday night at area truck stops; weigh station records for trucks passing through the state; neighbors to be re-interviewed; landscaping, roofing, and painting crews that worked in her neighborhood in the last three months…" He set his elbows on the desk and shook his head. "And the damn chief wants every lead run down and a report filed for him to review. It can't be done."

"It can be done but not by one man," Pandori said.

"Not by ten officers," Nicoletti said. "At least not thoroughly and quickly."

"So what do you suggest?" Reichert looked at Nicoletti.

"Lenny submits the ViCAP report and handles all the follow-up. You concentrate on anyone who surfaced in Marie-Justine's life in the forty-eight hours before her death."

"You were all around her in her last forty-eight hours," Reichert asserted once again.

"Then go back three days, a week if you have to. I'll bet somewhere this killer crossed her path, and there is someone out there who saw it and can give you a description of him." Nicoletti started to leave the room.

"Where are you going?" Pandori asked.

"I've got an appointment. I'll call you later. Reichert, don't lose heart. Statistically, the name of the killer will be in your files within the first thirty days of the investigation. Your job is to recognize it when you see it."

"And just how am I supposed to recognize it?"

"No one really knows," Nicoletti said as he walked down the hall. "But if you're lucky, the name will come to you from more than one source."

Reichert looked at Pandori. "What the hell is he talking about?"

FORTY-FIVE

Anne Bertone, wearing jeans and the same green Colorado State sweatshirt she wore the first time he saw her at the café, met Nicoletti at his hotel precisely at twelve thirty. She drove him to Marie-Justine's house and parked her green Blazer in the empty driveway.

Standing in the kitchen, Nicoletti was numb. He could not focus on Anne Bertone's voice. He looked through the window framed by yellow-and-white curtains. Nicoletti stared at the garden but saw nothing.

In his hands, he held a photocopy of Marie-Justine's letter. His eyes blurred with tears he willed not to fall. He handed the letter back to Anne, who slid it into a large folder in the center of the small oak table. He imagined it was the same table where Marie-Justine had translated her emotions into writing two nights earlier.

Nicoletti went into the living room and found a photograph of a younger Dr. Junot with his arms around his daughter.

"I didn't know what to think," Anne said. "Frankly, I still don't. I checked with my sources, and every one of them praised your investigative instincts; my DEA sources in Denver all claimed you are one of the best.

"I talked to Lenny Pandori early this morning. He said you solved a murder case in Atlanta when he was assigned there as well as several others around the country. Said that without your efforts, the killers would have never been discovered. He's the one who suggested that I contact you. He believes that Chief Garland is ignoring other possibilities and is only looking in one direction for M-J's murderer—and that direction leads to you."

Nicoletti returned to the kitchen. "Garland has no choice. He has to go with the facts as they develop, and at this point, most of the evidence puts me in the middle of this.

"If you look at it objectively, from the point of view of statistics, the murderer is generally found in the vicinity of the victim within twenty-four hours prior to the murder. I'm the one who appears to have been stalking Justine all day Saturday. I was with her Saturday night and all day Sunday.

"Except for the killer, I was most likely the last person to see her alive. My fingerprints, my vest, my pen were all around her the night she was murdered. What else can Garland do? He has to stick to what the circumstances and the evidence tell him." He rested his arms on the table. "If I were in his place, I'd probably do the same thing."

"I've read M-J's letter a dozen times. You could not have fooled her like that. Her father told me he knows you are innocent. He made me promise to help you." Anne took a deep breath. "There has to be more. If you didn't do it, then there has to be something Garland and Reichert are overlooking. That's why I brought you here. That's why Pandori gave me these reports he got from Reichert this morning." She tapped her hand on the folder in front of her.

Nicoletti pulled the file across the table. There was nothing new in the pages he reviewed. When he looked up, Anne was placing a blue ceramic mug of Earl Grey tea in front of him. He clasped it in both hands, grateful for the warmth.

He was ready to begin. He pushed the file away and took a notebook and pen from his briefcase. "Tell me everything you can think of that might be important. I'm looking for someone, a male in his thirties, maybe a little older, who attached himself to you or Justine. Someone she dated, flirted with, a co-worker, a student. Maybe even someone as insignificant as a laborer hired to rake leaves in her yard."

"I don't know... Where should I begin?"

"Anywhere. Just start talking."

Anne began with her own arrival in Missoula. She had taken a sabbatical from *The Denver Post*, designed to give her time to write a novel about her grandmother, who had taken over the family's Montana ranch after her great-grandfather's death in the First World War.

He guided her to describe her relationship with Marie-Justine.

They had been roommates. From college through graduate school, they were inseparable. Anne had studied journalism and took a job at the Newark *Star-Ledger*, while Marie-Justine, with an advanced degree in genetics, moved to California to work on a project for an international biogenetic research firm.

According to Anne, as soon as Marie-Justine landed in Los Angeles, she was taken under the protective wing of Dr. David Cantrell, a world-renowned heart surgeon.

Cantrell had known Marie-Justine since she was a teenager. He was a colleague of her father's, and she had grown up listening to them discuss medical theories after dinner at their home in Geneva. Cantrell, although twenty years her senior, adored Marie-Justine and frequently stopped in New York to take the two roommates from their dreary apartment near the Columbia campus to dazzling five-star dinners.

A year after her arrival in California, Marie-Justine and David Cantrell were married. The marriage lasted ten years but began to deteriorate early on as Marie-Justine began to feel more like a daughter than a wife.

"He began to smother her," Anne said. "He made all the decisions and expected her to acquiesce to all of them. There was nothing she wanted for materially, but she felt like a second-class citizen.

"She was always expected to walk three paces behind." Anne's voice changed pitch and snapped Nicoletti to attention. "She was every bit as bright as he. Hell, she was brilliant. There was nothing she couldn't do." Anne paused. "Then the affairs began."

FORTY-SIX

"Enough," Nicoletti said, putting to an end Anne's description of the details of Marie-Justine's unfortunate marriage.

He was satisfied that an evil shadow from a dark corner of Marie-Justine's distant past had most likely not manifested itself in Missoula to take her life.

"Let's focus on her arrival in Missoula."

"But we can't ignore that Cantrell could be a suspect," she said.

"Cantrell might have reason enough to want her out of his life, but wanting her dead is another matter. You don't like him, I get it, but that isn't enough to justify wasting time on speculation."

Reluctantly, Anne resumed her narrative. Marie-Justine's move to Missoula provided a physical break from her life with Cantrell. She had arranged to take a position in the biological sciences department at the university. Upon her arrival, she moved in with Anne. That lasted for about two months, until she purchased the yellow-and-white cottage.

"She was so happy here. Every day she grew more radiant." Anne sipped her second cup of tea.

The phone rang. From the living room they could hear Marie-Justine's recorded voice on the answering machine, happily inviting the caller to leave a message. There was no message. The line went dead.

"I hate it when that happens," Anne said. "I used to get those hang-up calls all the time. M-J used to say it was my secret admirer. It seemed like whenever I would leave the house, there would be two or three of those messages waiting for me when I got back. Then, one day they just stopped."

"Did the police listen to this tape?" Nicoletti said as he walked into the living room and stood over the recorder next to the phone.

"It's not a tape; it's digital."

"Did they listen to it?"

"Yes, Garland listened to it several times, but there is nothing on it just two messages from me from last weekend."

"Maybe he listened to it but never really heard it."

Nicoletti pushed the message replay button.

The first message was from Anne on Saturday, telling Marie-Justine she would be at the café at ten as planned.

The next three callers left no message.

Then they listened to the message Anne left on Sunday while Marie-Justine and Nicoletti were hiking. Anne turned away as she heard her own voice talking to her dearest friend, who would be dead several hours later.

Then there were another series of hang-up calls, ending with the one they had just received.

Nicoletti started the messages again. He skipped past Anne's first call and listened to the first three hang-ups. He narrowed his focus on the second call in the series. They listened to it several times more.

"You hear that, right?" he asked Anne. "In the background of that call, it's the sound of a siren."

"Yes, I heard it. But the caller doesn't say anything. It sounds like he just slammed the phone down."

"In all the other calls, there is no delay in the caller hanging up. As soon as the call is connected to the recorder, the line goes dead. But in that one call, whoever it was allowed the recording to begin before they disconnected. Then, as if angry or in a panic, they slammed down the receiver."

"I wouldn't read too much into it. Like I said, we used to get those calls all the time at my place. After M-J moved, she started to get them here too."

"And you said you don't get them anymore?"

"They tapered off, then one day they just stopped."

"Before or after Marie-Justine moved out?" He realized that he was beginning to call her by her full name. He hoped it was not a sign that his connection to Justine was beginning to leave his consciousness.

"After, I guess. She started getting similar calls here and mine stopped. I remember we joked that my secret admirer had decided to dump me for her." Anne smiled.

Nicoletti was not smiling. "Let's take a break." He abruptly started for the front door. "We can go to the café on Arthur Avenue."

"What's the matter?"

"I can't think. Something is pressing on my brain. I have to get out of here."

FORTY-SEVEN

They ordered coffee. Nicoletti was relieved to be outside in the fresh air. He could not have stayed another minute in Marie-Justine's home. He needed a neutral place to clear his head. He sensed he was close to discovering something of consequence, but his logical mind could not capture it.

He did not know exactly what he was looking for. He was trying too hard. And he was not being good company for Anne. He sat silently in the chair at the café where he had been sitting Saturday morning when he first saw them.

At Nicoletti's request, Anne provided every detail she had regarding Marie-Justine's life at the university. He listened to every word but heard nothing that added to the solution he was seeking.

"Think back to Saturday morning. Was there anything about Marie-Justine's mood that you felt to be odd or troubling?"

"No, in fact, quite the opposite. The divorce was final. We laughed, talked, made plans for dinner. We talked about you."

"Me?"

"Yes, you. Why not? A good-looking stranger, with nothing better to do than stare at us? Of course we talked about you." She slapped the back of his hand.

"Did anyone know you were meeting her here?"

"No. Well, my friend Jim would have known. M-J and I came here every Saturday morning ever since she moved to Missoula. It was our little ritual. Why?"

Nicoletti shrugged; he had no answer. He was searching, moving every stone, looking for something he could not articulate.

He leaned back in the chair and lit a cigarette. "My turn," he said, thinking back to Saturday morning.

Methodically, he described to Anne his observations. He started with her arrival at the café—the crashing of her bicycle into the metal rack—then Justine sitting at the table alone, their greeting, the perfume, the laughter. He pictured the two women sitting in the sun. He saw Justine lean back, letting her hair fall behind the chair. He recalled the waitress, the young man with the camera, the incessant clicking of the shutter.

He stopped talking and strained his memory. There was something; he knew something.

Then he saw it. The hand. He saw it come from nowhere, moving out to touch the chestnut braid. The hand was awkwardly protruding from the sleeve of a gray coat. He remembered that it went inside the restaurant, then quickly returned to the patio. The hand again reached for Justine's hair but was foiled in its mission when she abruptly leaned forward as if to avoid the object she could not even see. The man in the gray coat crossed the street and walked into the dormitory. Nicoletti again felt the primal urge to attack.

"Crossing the street... the ambulance."

"What? Who's crossing the street? What ambulance?"

"The guy was on the phone, over there." He pointed to the pay phone on the other side of Arthur Avenue. "He had slammed down the receiver as the ambulance went by."

Nicoletti stood up, took Anne by the arm, and led her across the patio to the table under the purple-and-green umbrella.

"Sit here," he said as he pushed her into the seat Marie-Justine had occupied. He hurried across the street to the phone. He picked up the receiver and looked back at the café.

A bewildered Anne hesitantly returned his wave, apparently pushed off balance by the sudden and unexpected animation of a man who had barely moved a muscle in the last twenty minutes.

He walked back to the café and put a tip under the edge of his coffee cup. Then he took Anne's hand and pulled her to her feet. "Come on. Let's walk back to Justine's and get your Blazer. I need a ride to the airport. I need a rental car."

"What's going on?" she asked as he pulled her along the uneven sidewalk.

"I'll explain as we go. I'm going to need Pandori to do some checking for me." He picked up his pace. "Do you have a gun?"

"Yes. At home."

"Do you know how to use it?"

"I grew up on a ranch in Montana. What do you think?"

FORTY-EIGHT

The last customer of the day was leaving. Charles Durbin smiled at the pretty blonde as she loaded her six-year-old golden retriever into the back of a station wagon. He waved as the blonde got behind the wheel and drove away.

"That one would do nicely. She's pretty and clean. Maybe I should consider her before I leave. But not now; I'm previously committed. And a gentleman doesn't cheat on his lady," Durbin proclaimed to an empty house. He locked the front door and finished cleaning the grooming area.

In the kitchen, he poured chilled chardonnay into a pewter-stemmed glass. He hummed along with the melancholy refrain from a new Sting CD as he slowly climbed the wide wooden stairs for a well-earned shower.

The last few days had been exhilarating but exhausting. He had forced himself to keep up his work schedule. He knew the police would be looking for anyone who failed to show up for work or left town unexpectedly. A least that is what he had read. Whether the police in

Missoula would be knowledgeable enough to make that type of inquiry, he doubted, but he was not one to take any chances.

He leaned against the tile in the shower. The music and the sound of the water lulled him into a mild trance. The hot water beat against his back as he recalled his night with Marie-Justine. He moved his hands along his thighs. His excitement increased as he focused on his silent approach.

He remembered coming up behind her in the dark. He recalled the look of terror on her face as she turned to find him already upon her. At first she seemed confused. Then there was a hint of recognition followed by fear. The beauty of her eyes when she realized his intent.

He had swiftly moved against her, spinning her around, putting his gloved hand under her chin and raising her head for the noose. Her face... her face... He closed his eyes, squeezing them tightly, straining to recall her face.

All he could see was the face of Dr. Kimba.

The spell was broken.

Dr. Kimba had spoiled his conquest. He had ruined the images of his victory. Dr. Kimba's pathetic, emaciated face and his bony hands, with their paper-thin skin, were all that Durbin could see.

"What right does that quack have to interfere with the memories of my achievement?" Durbin screamed in the tile and glass enclosure. "It was because of him that I rushed to her too soon. It could have been so magnificent." Durbin reached down and took hold of himself, exerting pressure to the point of pain. "She should have been brought here, where we could have taken time to enjoy the moment fully." He released his grasp. "My work is not finished. I will conquer again, and this time, there will be no Dr. Kimba—no one to interfere with my mind, my victory."

Durbin folded the damp towel and hung it on a heated rack. He brushed his short brown hair and then posed in the nude in front of the mirror. He was pleased with what he saw.

He walked across the highly polished, blond wood floor to the master bedroom closet and carefully selected a wardrobe suited for his night's work: forest-green work pants, a black T-shirt, and a black hooded sweatshirt. He set each garment on the bed. He then chose dark brown hiking boots and set them next to the nightstand.

He carried the wine glass by its pewter stem and crossed the hall into the guest room. He sat in the over-sized rocking chair next to the window and looked at the late afternoon light accentuating the texture of the heavy plaster on the faux-painted wall behind the bed.

He took a sip of the cool wine and crossed to the other side of the room to stand in front of a large oil painting. He touched the painting, allowing his fingertips to trace the outline of the woman. Her beautiful face was framed by an abundance of black hair that was pulled to one side and held with a large silver comb. The artist had taken great care to give the comb the same luminescence as her green eyes.

Durbin maintained contact with the green eyes that followed him as he walked naked about the room. Her lips were full and red, as if stained with pomegranate juice. A muted variation of the deep red accentuated her high cheekbones.

"I'm really glad we kept the beige, tan, and brown colors in this room," Durbin said to the painting. "It seems much more classical than the pale greens and yellows Marie-Justine used in her bedroom."

Durbin ran the fingers of his right hand along the red choker that was painted across the olive skin of the woman's neck. He let his thumb trace the fall of her neckline as it moved beneath the fluid folds of her red sarong, which was decorated with small golden dragons.

"We may be leaving here soon," he said as he traced the lower curve of the painting's right breast. "I know I promised that we would stay, that I would stop causing us difficulties, but this is not my fault."

He stepped to the dresser and opened the top drawer. He gently entwined a pair of woman's underpants in his left hand and raised the lacy garment to his face. He inhaled deeply, then replaced the item and closed the drawer.

"I'm going to be late tonight. Don't wait up. I'll try not to wake you when I get in." He pulled the door closed behind him.

He dressed slowly. From the closet, he chose a black coat. Before closing the door, he reached in and touched the shoulder of the gray parka. "I know you want to go, but you've been out far too much lately."

FORTY-NINE

Nicoletti parked the rental car and walked the last block to Anne Bertone's house. He struggled with the decision as to what to do next.

The statement he submitted to Detective Reichert had been as accurate as he had been able to make it. But now he was aware of additional information—things he had observed on Saturday morning that he had forgotten, observations that were recalled because of the sound of the siren on Marie-Justine's message machine.

The recording was evidence that Reichert needed to collect as soon as possible. He thought about calling him but figured Reichert might overreact to the idea of Nicoletti actively working on the case. And there would be hell to pay if Garland knew Nicoletti had been inside Marie-Justine's home.

He could truthfully say no one had told him to stay out of the house, but that was a weak and indefensible excuse for entering a possible crime scene. It was better to not press his luck. He decided to call Pandori and let him suggest to Reichert the seizure of the recording as evidence.

He also decided to continue to delay reporting the details of his observations concerning the man in the gray coat as well as the man on the pay phone across from the café. Was he an associate of Gray Coat's or Gray Coat himself? He needed more information. Once he got it, he would talk to Reichert.

Anne met him at the door, handed him a glass of red wine, and immediately took him on a tour of her home. The layout was similar to Marie-Justine's—all on one floor, master bedroom and connecting bath off the living room, a guest suite beyond the kitchen and pantry.

"Come in here," she said as she walked into her bedroom. "I want you to see this." She took a .38 caliber revolver from the nightstand and handed it to Nicoletti.

"Smith and Wesson, two-inch barrel, five shot." He opened the cylinder to be sure it was loaded. "I carried one like this for years as a backup gun. Very reliable." He handed it back to her.

"I thought you'd approve," Anne said, returning the weapon to the drawer.

"Until this is over, I want you to keep that gun with you at all times. It'll do you no good if you're downtown and it's in the bedroom."

"I usually keep it in my car or my purse. I just didn't think I'd need it in my apron while I cooked dinner."

"The heavy plaster on the wall behind the bed is a nice touch," he said, looking around the room.

"I took a class on plastering and faux painting. Thought I'd try it out. M-J picked out the colors for the paint. We did it while she was living here last summer."

She led the way back to the kitchen. "I wanted a rose tint, but she insisted on beige and brown."

Nicoletti set his wine glass on the kitchen counter. He studied the art deco stem of the glass. "Is this silver?"

"No, they're pewter." Anne placed a sheet of paper in front of him. "Pandori dropped this off about an hour ago. He said three calls were made to M-J's from the pay phone on Arthur Avenue on Saturday morning. He wanted to know what we had going. I told him I didn't know; he'd have to talk to you."

Nicoletti tried to contain the dinner conversation to disclosures about Anne's life and work, but she used the opportunity to discuss his life. He abandoned his usually vague responses and answered her directly. He liked her no-nonsense, matter-of-fact approach.

"I didn't offend you by checking up on you, did I?" She sounded a bit guilty.

"No, I was just surprised Lenny Pandori's word wasn't good enough for you."

"You know how we reporters are, always getting at least two sources. Besides, Lenny is not exactly an unbiased source. After all, you did save his life."

"Well, Tom Marley isn't exactly unbiased either."

"He called you?"

"Like I said, he's not an unbiased source."

"How so?" she asked.

"He's married to the daughter of my old partner, Bob McDermott."

"The one who was murdered?"

"How'd you—"

"Lenny told me about that. It must have been awful."

"It was a long time ago."

"Lenny said they never caught the murderer."

Nicoletti did not answer. He held his wine glass up to the overhead light, then swirled the dark red liquid around the side of the glass before taking a drink.

"Lenny said he's the one who introduced you to your wife." Anne changed the subject.

"That's not exactly true." Nicoletti smiled at Anne to reassure her that she had not blundered by bringing up other painful memories from his past. "Kristen was the attending physician at George Washington University Hospital the night Lenny got shot. Lenny was unconscious when I met her. She worked on him for about two hours before he stabilized."

"So she saved his life, not you."

"That's what I've always said. I guess he deserves credit for getting Kristen and me together. If he hadn't been so stupid, he would have never gotten shot." Nicoletti smiled. "Lenny was in the hospital for three weeks. I only visited him when I knew Kristen was on duty."

"How long were you married?"

"Twenty-three years."

"Kids?"

"Three. The oldest, Kristy, is twenty-two, works in New York City for *The Times*. The other two, both boys, are still in college, senior and sophomore years."

"How did your wife die?" Anne put her fork and knife down.

"Brain aneurysm. We were driving home from a dinner party. She had had a terrible headache all day. She leaned her head against the window and I thought she'd fallen asleep. By the time we got to the hospital, she was gone."

Anne changed the subject altogether and queried Nicoletti in areas as far away from Kristen as she could.

She found it odd that he cared for neither cars nor organized sports. She tested his French and found it sorely lacking.

"M-J used to criticize my French," she said. "You must have really swept her off her feet, or she would have run screaming from the room after listening to you."

His knowledge of art and literature impressed her.

"Even more so, considering your profession," she said as she poured the after-dinner coffee.

"What does my profession have to do with it?" He dropped two lumps of sugar and a splash of cream into the steaming cup.

"Well, you know, crime, investigations, 'hunting men,' as you so graphically put it… I just find it interesting that you have so many refined tastes and talents for a man of violence."

He tried to think of something to say to change the subject, but he wasn't quick enough.

"Apart from that time with Lenny, did you ever have to kill anyone else?"

"You never have to kill. You can always opt to sacrifice yourself to the sanctity of life. Now, tell me about your—"

"Did you ever kill anyone else?"

FIFTY

"Well, have you?" Anne waited for an answer.

"Yes."

"More than one other?"

"Yes."

"Was it difficult?"

"No."

"No?"

"I suppose I should say it was horrible, that I haven't felt the same since, and that I wake up at night surrounded by the faces of the dead." He paused and stared at her dark eyes. "But the truth is, when you go to work carrying a badge and a gun, you get it in your mind that you may have to take someone's life, you imagine how you are going to do it, and when that moment comes, you do it. You pull the trigger and keep pulling it until they go down. Sometimes they live; sometimes they die. That's it."

"How does it make you feel?"

"It makes you feel good that they're dead and you're not."

"Nothing else?"

"That's it. Nothing more," he lied.

A face spurting blood onto a predawn Parisian street started to form in his mind. He pushed it away as he often had to do with the others. He started to talk. He needed to create noise to chase away his memories.

"After it's over, there is one more thing." He tried to get more analytical. "You catalog in your mind the sequence of events and the justification for the shooting. Because you are going to have to explain the whole thing to the police and, later, to the prosecutors assigned to review the incident." He stopped talking. He had nothing more to say, and the faces of death were gone.

"Thank you," she said softly and leaned back in her chair. "Thank you for telling me."

There was a tone of seriousness in her voice that Nicoletti found curious.

They were quiet for a while. He picked up the dishes and brought them to her at the sink. He divided the remaining wine between their two glasses.

"The dinner was really delicious. My compliments to the chef."

"It was a recipe of M-J's. She's a wonderful cook." Anne hesitated and looked down into the sink as if saddened by the realization that Marie-Justine no longer existed in the present tense. "Anyway, I thought it would be fitting to treat you to one of her favorites."

"I'm glad you did." He walked into the living room and took a deep breath of the night air blowing in through the large open windows. "It is pretty dark out there. Want me to close the windows?"

"No, thanks. I like to leave the windows open when the weather is nice like this." She dried her hands on a towel. "During the warm months, I keep all the windows open. I love the feel of the night breeze."

"Well, I don't want to change your lifestyle, but it would be best to shut things down at night. You know… for safety." He walked back into the kitchen.

"I suppose you're right, but I hate to do it. I kept the house closed up when I first moved here, coming from Denver and all. But after M-J moved in, we got in the habit of keeping the place as open as possible."

"You know, living alone, have you ever thought about getting a dog? They're a great early warning system in the event of uninvited guests."

"I did when I first moved in, then forgot about it until M-J got here. We talked about getting all kinds of dogs. I even went so far as to leave my name with a dog groomer on the other side of town that a neighbor recommended. She told me he sometimes gets great dogs from his customers—you know, people who are moving or getting too old to take care of them. So I went over there and talked to him. He said he'd keep an eye out and let me know. But it never worked out."

"He probably lost your name as soon as you left."

"No, he actually came by one day with a beautiful golden retriever. He said the owners were thinking of giving her up and asked if I would be interested. But by that time, M-J was getting ready to move out and I had gotten used to the house—you know, no longer spooked by every creak in the night. So I thanked him, told him I wasn't ready to commit to a long-term relationship with a pet, and that was that."

Nicoletti pulled a pack of cigarettes from his pocket. "I'm going to step out on your back porch."

"You can smoke in here."

"Thanks, but I'd rather be outside."

"It's through the guest bedroom."

Nicoletti walked off, searching his pockets for a match.

"The porch light is burned out, so be careful. And no need to lecture me on the importance of exterior lighting, Mr. Safety. I've already bought the replacement bulbs. I just haven't got around to it yet."

Anne hardly had time to put the roasting pan away before Nicoletti was back in the kitchen.

"Decided to take my offer to stay inside?"

He walked past her and systematically shut and locked every window in the house. When he returned to the kitchen, he turned off the lights near the sink and over the table, leaving the lamp in the living room to illuminate them in the dimmest of light.

He pulled her firmly against his chest.

"What the hell are you doing?"

"Take this and put it in your waistband." He thrust the gun he had taken from the nightstand into her hand. "There is someone standing behind the trees outside the kitchen window. I'm going to leave—"

"Leave? Leave me here? Alone?" She struggled to get the gun between her shirt and her jeans.

"Be quiet and listen." He moved between Anne and the kitchen window. "I am going to leave. Wait two minutes, then go out the front door and get in your car. Have your keys ready so you can get in and start it and get going right away. Drive past M-J's house, then across the Higgins Street Bridge. Go to my hotel and park under the portico at the lobby entrance. Go inside and wait for me. No matter what, don't leave until I get there." He started toward the door. "Keep your cell phone on. Call mine if there's a problem."

"If there's a problem…" she grumbled as Nicoletti left her behind.

She took a dark coat from the closet, placed her cell phone in the front pocket, and picked up her car keys. Moving to the front door, she looked down at the floor, the rugs, the baseboards, never allowing her eyes to drift up in the direction of the windows. She felt cold. She was afraid. She was alone.

FIFTY-ONE

Durbin forced himself to calm down. He had been infuriated at the sight of Nicoletti embracing Anne. When they left her house, he had followed them. Why? What was he going to do? He hadn't decided.

He gradually accelerated, closing the distance between the Suburban and Anne's car. She was alone. Where was Nicoletti?

In the rearview mirror, he saw headlights. Was this a trap?

Durbin forced the Suburban into an abrupt right turn and raced down the block. As he came to a stop sign, he looked back. The headlights were turning behind him. He stepped on the gas.

He never acted without a plan and now he was paying the price for his uncontrolled behavior. After a series of senseless turns, the headlights disappeared. He was confident he was no longer being followed but not sure enough to go directly home.

It had been foolish to follow Anne. How did he allow Nicoletti to vanish? No matter. Now he needed to recover. First, he needed to establish a reason for being on the street.

Durbin drove into the parking lot behind police headquarters and parked in one of the spaces reserved for police vehicles. There were no headlights to be seen. Had he only imagined someone had been following him? Now he saw nothing suspicious. He held his breath, closed his eyes, and listened. He heard nothing.

As usual, the rear entrance was propped open with a block of wood. Durbin pulled the door and kicked the wood aside as he entered. Sergeant Tom Sheppard was standing a few yards from the door, pinning something on a bulletin board.

"Hey, Charlie, what brings you here this time of night?"

"Hi, Sarge. I'm looking for Tim Sloan."

"He's out with the narcs tonight. What do you need?"

"Nothing important. I was just planning on taking a vacation and thought he might want to bring Champ in for a grooming before I left."

"Leave him a note in his box in the roll-call room. There's paper and pencils on the podium."

Durbin walked down the hall, past the break room where two men he didn't recognize were sitting at the round Formica table.

In the roll-call room, he stood at the podium and scribbled a note. He was looking for Sloan's mailbox when he heard a low moan from across the hall. The moan repeated, this time a little louder. He recognized the sound—it was a dog. More than a dog, it was a hound.

He threw the note on the podium and looked around. There was no exit door. He had to go back the way he came.

Quickly, he moved down the hall. A few feet more and he would be around the corner and out the back door. Turning his head to look behind him as he made the corner, he saw the bloodhound emerge from the break room. Nose to the floor, it headed into the roll-call room.

Two men were in the hall, standing between Durbin and the door.

"Get squared away, Charlie?" Sergeant Sheppard said.

"Just fine, Sarge." Durbin pushed past them without slowing down. Slamming the door behind him, he broke into a run toward the Suburban.

"Who was that?" Detective Reichert asked.

"Some dog groomer looking for Sloan. He does some work on the K-9s. He's a friend of the chief's wife. It was her idea to hire him."

"How did he get in here?"

"The back door was propped open."

"For Chrissake," Reichert mumbled. "They pay to put in a security door that's never locked, and they waste good money on bullshit just because the chief's wife suggests it. What a place."

.   .   .

Durbin drove for ten minutes on the busiest streets he could find, trying desperately to bury his scent amid the traffic and shopping centers. When he had gone as far as he felt was necessary, he doubled back. His clothing, especially his boots, had to be destroyed. Tonight.

FIFTY-TWO

"Who is he? What was he doing at my house?"

"That's what we're going to find out."

Anne struggled to hook her seat belt as Nicoletti drove out of the hotel parking lot.

"I think we're okay. He started to follow you, but once you got into town, he dropped off. I followed him to the police station and watched him go in the back door. Garland must have assigned him to keep an eye on you."

"Or keep an eye on *you*."

"He wasn't following me."

"What did he look like?"

"I didn't get a good look at him, but—"

Nicoletti's cell phone rang.

"Hey … Okay. What about Reichert? … Don't bother. I'm at police headquarters now. I'll ask him myself. Thanks." He snapped the phone shut. "That was Lenny. Garland didn't assign anyone to follow you… or me."

•   •   •

Retired Sergeant Bennigan came out the back door and was pulled by his dog across the parking lot. Reichert watched from the open door.

"What's that all about?" Nicoletti said to Reichert as the dog circled the space where the gray Suburban had been parked. He saw Anne twisting in the rental to watch the dog in action.

"Hell if I know," Reichert said. "The dog has been sniffing his way up and down the halls and in and out of offices for the last ten minutes. Finally, he ended up at the back door and started howling. Probably has to shit."

"Look, Reichert, I know it's none of my business, but do you have someone following me or Anne Bertone?"

"You're right; it's none of your business."

Nicoletti waited.

"Fact of the matter is, I don't have anyone in this department I would trust to follow a bakery truck around town."

"You have anyone who drives a gray Suburban?"

"The chief has one, but it's dark green."

"A gray Suburban followed Anne Bertone tonight. I saw it park in this lot, right where that dog is circling. The driver went in this door about fifteen minutes ago."

"Come inside."

FIFTY-THREE

Nicoletti parked the rental car in the shifting shadow of a large elm tree. "Stay here." He took the piece of paper on which Reichert had scribbled the address.

Anne shivered as she watched him walk down the street and disappear, eventually returning from the alley behind the house.

"The Suburban is parked in the alley," he said.

"Are you sure it's the same one?"

"Lock the car and follow me. It's the third house from the corner."

It was a large Victorian-style house with turrets forming the upper-front rooms on either side of the façade. A light was on in one of the upstairs rooms. A silhouetted figure moved behind the curtains.

They walked in silence toward the house. A strong wind blew against their faces and rustled the leaves in the large trees that hovered over the sidewalk. The movement of leaves and branches scattered the light from the streetlamps and shifted shadows all around them.

Anne clutched Nicoletti's arm as they approached the front of the Victorian. A carved wooden sign in the front yard identified the house as the *Montana Salon for Pets*.

"I can't believe it," Anne said as soon as they got back in the car. "That's the place, the dog groomer I called—the one who brought the dog to the house."

Nicoletti had figured as much when he first saw the sign in the yard. He had not told Anne of his conclusion because he wanted her to see the house with fresh eyes. He wanted her reaction to be spontaneous.

Anne looked back at the house as they drove away. "I lied about the windows," she said. "About always keeping them open. I wanted to sound fearless. A few days after he brought the dog, he showed up again. M-J was home alone; I had gone on a camping trip with my friend Jim. She told me the dog guy had stopped by to see if we had reconsidered getting a dog. M-J said he gave her the creeps. From that day on, M-J closed and locked all the windows and doors at the first hint of twilight."

Nicoletti was relieved that Marie-Justine's intuition had not failed her. He wondered how she could have been caught by surprise that night by the river.

He pulled up to Anne's Blazer in the parking lot of the hotel. "Can you get Jim to stay at your place for the next few days?"

"He's out of town until next week."

"Well, you should be fine. It looks like the dog guy is down for the night. I'll follow you home, then go back to the hotel and call you first thing in the morning."

"Fuck you will, Nicoletti. My hard-nosed reporter act only goes so far. I don't give a shit if you stand next to my bed and blow cigarette smoke in my face all night. I'm not staying alone."

FIFTY-FOUR

Nicoletti spent Thursday morning making calls from Anne Bertone's kitchen table. By ten o'clock, he had set things in motion.

His first call was to the senior partner of the law firm in Washington. After he explained why he had to delay his return to work, the partner had insisted on putting him in touch with a defense attorney in Helena, who had then referred Nicoletti to Robert Marx, a local attorney in Missoula.

Marx was familiar with the case and wanted to meet right away before Nicoletti "answered any more questions from the police." Nicoletti put off the meeting until Friday. He did not want to waste several hours listening to a lawyer articulate the obvious.

The Missoula attorney was pacified when Nicoletti agreed Marx could immediately notify Chief Garland that Nicoletti was now represented by counsel and the police should refrain from contacting his client directly.

After being safely nestled into the cocoon of that part of the justice system reserved for the accused, Nicoletti went about his work as the investigator, a role with which he was, thankfully, more familiar. In between calls, he paced from room to room, waiting for the results to trickle in.

Thomas Marley was the first to call back. The DEA computer operators in Denver had found the Montana license plate on the 1999 Chevrolet Suburban registered to Charles Durbin. The address on the registration was the same as the one Reichert had supplied last night, and it was the same address the local phone book listed for the *Montana Salon for Pets*.

Anne came through the front door with Lenny Pandori. In the kitchen, Nicoletti was pouring his fifth cup of coffee and finishing his third cell phone call with Marley. To Nicoletti, Pandori looked younger and more energized than he had the day before at the police station.

"Nico, pour me a cup." Pandori sat at the table and handed Nicoletti several pieces of paper.

The first sheet confirmed, through the Montana Department of Motor Vehicles, the information Marley had provided. The second was a faxed copy of Durbin's driver's license photo, which Anne identified as the dog groomer. The third sheet was an addendum to the license and registration information, indicating that Durbin had been previously licensed in the state of Colorado.

Nicoletti's cell phone rang. It was Marley again.

"Hey, Nico, I did some more checking. There was a Charles Durbin in the system who has a prior arrest in Colorado Springs, September third of last year. He was charged with criminal trespassing. The printout doesn't show the final disposition of the case, but the date of birth and the description match your Durbin."

"Get a hold of Ken Palmer in the Springs," Nicoletti said.

"Ken retired last year. There's a new guy running the DEA office now, a guy out of headquarters."

"No. I don't want any new guys. Call Palmer. I need an old-timer I can trust. Brief him on the situation. Give him the information you found and ask him to run it all down. When he has something solid, tell him to call me on my cell."

"Yes, sir. Once a general, always a general. I'll call you later."

Nicoletti turned his attention to Pandori. "How far along is Reichert?"

"Not very—he's buried in paper and leads. They've added two investigators from the sheriff's department to help on the case, but Garland has them following up on the out of town truckers they've identified by gasoline receipts."

"Did he pick up Marie-Justine's answering machine?"

"Yesterday afternoon. I went with him right after I got the call from you. He kept asking why I thought it was so important. All I told him was that we had to be thorough in case it became important later."

"And that was good enough?"

"No, but he's so overwhelmed that any questions he has in his mind only stay there for a few seconds, then he forgets about them."

"That's not good," Nicoletti said. "If he's going to find the killer, he's got to keep thinking clearly. Nothing should be forgotten and fall through the cracks. I'm going to talk to Chief Garland. He's got to get the sheriff's office fully involved. Reichert needs all the help he can get."

"I don't think *you* talking to Chief Garland about anything right now is a good idea." Pandori got up and poured another cup of coffee. "Garland still sees you as the most likely perpetrator. He's not going to take any chance that could lead the press to believe he's taking investigative advice from his prime suspect."

"That's ridiculous."

"Think so? They had a press conference this morning. Deputy Chief McKay told them the police had several suspects, some of whom had already been interviewed."

"Who else has been interviewed?" Anne asked.

"Only our boy Nico, no one else," Pandori said. "So you can see that Garland is already setting the stage for a quick arrest."

Anne opened the refrigerator and took out a pitcher of iced tea. "That's the dumbest thing he could do. If the press is expecting an immediate arrest, every day that goes by will make them more aggressive. In a week, they'll be demanding Garland's head on a plate."

"Garland's got other pressures to worry about," Pandori said. "I was in his office this morning when the DA stopped in. Garland told him that the fingerprints were a match to Nico's. They agreed that if the blood type on the down vest found near Marie-Justine's body is also a match, and they can get a positive identification from a lineup, they won't wait for DNA results before arresting Nico."

"And what was supposed to be my motive?" Nicoletti said.

"They'll invent one if they have to just to get the thing resolved," Pandori said. "I told you, Nico, they don't care if they drop the charges later. The effort is not to have this hanging over any of their heads during the campaign."

"Well, they're not going to get the lineup ID any time soon. My lawyer, Robert Marx, will see to that."

"Marx?" Pandori said. "You gotta be kiddin'. That poor bastard couldn't shake a turd off a stick, let alone get anyone off a murder charge."

Nicoletti swallowed hard. He sat at the table and rubbed his right shoulder. "What else?" he asked Pandori.

"The only other avenue that Garland is allowing Reichert to pursue is the possibility that Dr. David Cantrell might have hired someone to kill Marie-Justine." Pandori took a sip of coffee. "The problem is that Reichert doesn't have time to piss, let alone follow up on leads in California."

"Neither do we," Nicoletti said. "You know, Lenny, you can get jammed up by working with me behind Garland's back."

"The way I figure it, it's not behind his back; it's out in front of him. Besides, if the Bureau tries to transfer me for pissing off the local big wigs, I'm sure you can get that big law firm of yours to battle it as punitive in the DC, courts. By the time they finish filing the paperwork, I'll be ready to retire anyway."

"Maybe I could get Robert Marx to take your case."

"Yeah, with him representing me, I'll beat the transfer and end up on the guillotine." Pandori turned to Anne. "What was the color and type of clothing Marie-Justine wore most often?"

"I don't know," she said. "Maybe gray and black. Or blue jeans and white shirts. I don't know. Why?"

"It's part of the ViCAP form I'm filling out and I want to get it done today," Pandori said.

"ViCAP—what's that?" Anne asked.

"It's a crime analysis report for the Violent Criminal Apprehension Program," Nicoletti said. "Detectives who have homicides, solved or unsolved, that involve abductions or appear to be random or sexually oriented, submit the information to the program for analysis and comparison to other similar crimes in the system. If they find any significant matches, they notify the detectives so they can begin to share their information and evidence."

"Most serial killers develop patterns," Pandori said. "The sooner the facts of one homicide in a series can be linked to other crimes by the same killer, the sooner information can be developed to catch him before he claims more victims."

"You think M-J was murdered by a serial killer?" Anne looked at both men.

Pandori looked at Nicoletti, who was nodding his head affirmatively to Anne's question.

"Lenny, before you go back to the office, I need you to set up on Durbin's house. If he goes anywhere, give him a loose tail and keep me advised. I'll relieve you in about an hour."

Anne closed the front door behind Pandori and looked at Nicoletti. "What do we do now?" she asked.

"Let's go over to Marie-Justine's. You can check her closet for an accurate answer to the ViCAP question. Since we don't have any good information on the killer, the better we detail Marie-Justine, the better the analyst's response will be. Then you can come back here. I'll go back to the hotel to check messages, shower, change clothes, and then hook up with Lenny," he said.

She stood facing him with her hands on her hips. "What am I supposed to do while you two are out watching Durbin?"

"You stay here. Keep the doors locked and I'll call you later." He walked past her.

At the front door, he stopped and turned around. She had a look on her face that made Nicoletti glad she didn't have anything to throw at him.

"Okay, lock up the house. Grab some of that bottled water you've got stacked in your fridge and let's go. And you'd better take a coat. It's going to be a long night."

Anne hurried out the door and caught up with Nicoletti on the front walk.

"You're not quite the tough old bastard you think you are," she said.

FIFTY-FIVE

Nicoletti followed Anne into Marie-Justine's bedroom. The heavy plaster wall behind the headboard caught his eye.

"I think I like the colors on your wall better," he said.

"So did M-J. She was going to repaint that wall." Anne opened the closet and ran her hand across the clothes. "There's more blue here than I remembered." She started to laugh. "Will you look at this? I guess Miss Perfection must have let this slip."

"What is it?"

"This dress… It's hung the wrong way." Anne pulled a lavender dress from the closet. "M-J was always turning my dresses around on the hangers so that they all faced the same way. She used to—"

Nicoletti grabbed the dress from Anne and stared at the zipper. Attached to the top was a small turquoise star.

He carried the dress into the living room.

"The flowers in the glass vase by the door…" he said.

"I know they need more water. I saw that when we came in."

He pushed past Anne, handing her the dress as he went through the bedroom and into the bathroom. He reached down and turned on the night light near the baseboard. He saw his shadow, a distorted image across the tiled wall.

He stepped into the bedroom and looked at Anne. "He finally decided on Lady B."

"Who? Who's he? Who's Lady B?"

"Something Dr. Kimba said about one of his patients—a psycho fixated on two women."

Anne stared at him as if she was unable to process what he was saying.

"That leaves Lady A. Lady Anne." He pulled the cell phone from his belt and dialed.

"What's going on?" Anne asked.

Nicoletti held up his hand to silence her. "Lenny, it's Nico. I'm at Marie-Justine's. Get over here right away." He looked at Anne. "She's here, with me."

FIFTY-SIX

"And I'm telling you the Kimba case is closed." Chief Garland threw the file on his desk and looked hard at Nicoletti. "The medical examiner found the injuries consistent with a fall down a flight of stairs. The doctor's neck was broken during the fall. End of story."

"But suppose I'm right," Nicoletti said, "and Dr. Kimba was murdered to keep him from identifying his patient as Marie-Justine's killer. If you stop the investigation into Dr Kimba's death before you get a court order to look through his patient files, all you're doing is giving the killer time to get away or strike again."

"There is no mystery patient, no Mr. X."

"How do you know? Until you review the files—"

"I looked at the files. There were twenty-seven active files in Kimba's office, and none of them matched your Mr. X."

"I thought you were waiting for a court order."

"When the ME came back with a finding of accidental death, the chances of getting a warrant evaporated."

Garland sat on the corner of his desk. "I took a look at the files just in case the ME was wrong and you were right."

Nicoletti looked at the chief. He knew Garland had just admitted to the commission of a crime. The review of the doctor's files without court authorization could cost him his job, force his resignation, and end his political ambitions. Garland had just handed Nicoletti information that could be used against him, officially and unofficially. It was a sharing of a confidence that changed Nicoletti's opinion of the man and would change the nature of their relationship.

"So you do believe me."

"I don't know what to believe. The DA thinks you made up the whole Mr. X thing. Even if the medical examiner had ruled Dr. Kimba's death suspicious, he was ready to go with the theory that you're the killer and that something you said to Kimba made him suspicious of you. He thinks you went to Kimba's house, killed him to cover your tracks, and invented Kimba's concerns about his patient to send us on a wild goose chase."

"What about the flower vase, the dress, the nightlight in the bathroom? That proves the killer was stalking Marie-Justine. Add to that the posing of her body, the makeup, combing her hair, and the method of death. It all means you've got a serial killer, advanced in his technique and probably well on his way to killing again. Doesn't the DA give a shit about that?"

"We agree on the postmortem manipulation of the victim. As far as knowing about her house and clothing, those are things you could have seen on Sunday."

"Could have, but I didn't," Nicoletti said calmly. "What about Kimba's appointment book? We could match the entries to the patient files. If there is a name in the appointment book that does not have a matching file, it could be Mr. X."

"There is no appointment book," Garland said.

"Have you ever heard of a doctor who did not keep an appointment book?"

"No, that's why I'm not completely willing to accept Kimba's death as an accident," Garland said. "But the DA will explain it as part of your diabolical plan. You could have removed the appointment book to bolster the theory that there is a missing file."

"You were at the house when I left with Pandori. You didn't see me carry out any appointment book."

"You think that's going to influence the DA? He'll just go with the possibility that you went to the house, killed Kimba, then took the appointment book back to your hotel or threw it out along the way. Then you took a cab back to Kimba's house to establish a timeline and provide a witness to your arrival. Once you were back inside Kimba's, you talked to Pandori and waited for the rest of us to arrive."

"For Chrissake, why not theorize that the deaths were the work of aliens visiting Earth for a few days?"

"Because no one has seen any aliens around town, but plenty of people have seen you." Garland softened his voice. "Look, Nicoletti, I know it sucks. But I'm just telling you the way it is, but I'm still a cop who knows when something doesn't feel right. So if you've got any other ideas, I'm willing to listen."

Nicoletti thought of telling Garland about the gray coat, the phone calls from the pay phone, and Durbin standing outside Anne's house. He decided to wait, even though it made him feel guilty. Garland's sudden reasonableness wasn't guaranteed to continue beyond his last sentence.

"Why did you advise me not to talk directly to the press?" Garland asked.

"Because you are the top official in the department. By you discussing the case, you are granting the killer the satisfaction of knowing he is dealing with the boss. If he's ego-driven, it only rewards him when you are interviewed or quoted."

"Really?"

"Yeah. Have a captain or even a sergeant handle the press. Make the bastard feel like you think he's a piece of shit, not worthy of your attention."

The chief's phone rang. He picked it up and listened, then hung up. "I've got another appointment," Garland said as a way of dismissing Nicoletti. "Pandori is looking for you. He's in his office, upstairs."

Nicoletti made his way down the hall. A tall, elegant, gray-haired man with a dark tan and an expensive suit brushed past him. Over his shoulder, Nicoletti heard Chief Garland's greeting.

"Dr. Cantrell, thank you for coming. I'm sorry for your loss."

Nicoletti heard the chief's heavy wooden door close. He started up the staircase. At the first landing, he met Pandori.

"Hey, Nico, I've been looking for you. They just brought in a suspect."

"Is it Dr. Cantrell?" Nicoletti followed Pandori down the stairs.

"Cantrell? No. It's a local kid by the name of Benson. Tim Benson."

"A kid? How old is he?"

"Nineteen, maybe twenty. Reichert is interviewing him right now." Pandori stopped at the door to the interrogation room.

"That's too young," Nicoletti said.

"We'll see. Go up and wait in my office. I left the door open. I'll be back up after the initial questioning. Then we can go out to the crime scene, if you still want to."

"Nineteen is too young," Nicoletti said again.

FIFTY-SEVEN

Pandori was on his cell phone. Nicoletti was trying to skip a stone across the river.

"That was the FBI office in Billings. They've got two unsolved homicides of females in the last year: one was in her late twenties, the other in her mid-thirties. I'm going to drive down there tomorrow morning. I could use some company, if you want to go."

"I'm not going anywhere. Now, tell me about this Tim Benson kid." Nicoletti moved to the place where Marie-Justine's body was found.

"His name first came up when the cops were canvassing Marie-Justine's neighborhood. Apparently, Benson worked for a landscaper who had several customers in the area. Two of the customers lived down the street from Marie-Justine's house. Benson was on the crew that worked the neighborhood, so he could have spotted her after she moved in."

Nicoletti walked away from the bright sunlight into the shade of the trees and Pandori followed. "This is exactly where her body was found?"

"Yeah, her head was pointed north." Pandori gestured with his cell phone. "Benson is a local guy. Barely made it out of high school. Lots of problems—drugs, alcohol, a couple of fights in school, no long-term girl-friends. He works on a ranch outside of town and lives in the tack room of the stable, where I'm sure he's surrounded by nylon horse leads that could've been used to do the job."

"There are probably a hundred horse owners within twenty miles of here with access to the same type of stuff," Nicoletti said.

"Yeah, well, on the night of the murder, Benson was visiting his grandmother, who lives up there." Pandori pointed through the trees up a steep incline to a large house that overlooked the river.

"How do we know that?"

"The cops interviewed all the people living within two blocks of the river. One of the neighbors said they remembered the old lady's grandson's truck being parked in the driveway at about ten o'clock, and it was still there when the neighbor went to bed about midnight."

"What did Benson say?"

"He claims he went to his grandmother's at nine, had a few beers, watched television. Grandma went to bed about eleven. Benson said he had another beer, smoked a joint, and fell asleep on the couch, then woke up about one and went home. The grandmother confirms the story up until eleven. All she could add was that the kid was gone when she got up at five."

Nicoletti looked up the hill toward the grandmother's house. "I'm going up. Care to join me?"

"I couldn't make it up that hill even if I had two good legs. I'll wait right here."

Halfway up the hillside, Nicoletti stopped to catch his breath. He braced himself against a tree to keep from falling backward. Below, he heard Pandori talking on his phone.

"Nico," Pandori yelled. "Come on down. We have to go."

Sliding on pine needles and loose dirt, he traversed the hill from tree to tree until he had sideslipped and bumped his way back to Pandori. "There is no way anyone made it down that hill in the dark, at least not quietly enough to sneak up on Marie-Justine and take her by surprise." Nicoletti wiped sweat from the side of his face.

"Reichert just called. He wants us to meet him out at Benson's place."

"Us? Reichert wants us both to go?"

"He said Chief Garland told him to make sure I bring you." Pandori struggled on the inclined path from the river to the street. "He also said Tim Benson was arrested two years ago for rape."

"Was he convicted?"

"No, the case was dismissed. He was a juvenile and the court ordered the record sealed. It was just before Reichert was hired by the police department." Pandori stopped to catch his breath and rub his hip. "Garland was the lead investigator on the case."

FIFTY-EIGHT

Pandori turned onto a gravel road that passed between two large wooden pillars. Black wrought iron rods formed an arch connecting the pillars. Hanging from the arch was a sign indicating they were entering the *Lazy 7 Ranch*. A half mile later, the gravel road wound up a hillside and through a grove of trees. Nicoletti figured somewhere in the distance the gravel road led to a ranch house. They turned onto a dirt road and followed it for a mile before they saw the stables, which consisted of a large barn flanked by two long one-story structures.

All the buildings were painted a deep red with white trim. To the right was a training paddock enclosed by white fencing. Parked along the fence line were two marked cars: one from the police department, the other from the sheriff's office. In front of the barn door were two unmarked cars, both black Ford Expeditions.

Pandori parked next to the Expeditions. "Looks like Garland is here," he said as they got out and walked into the barn.

After stepping from the bright sunlight into the dark barn, Pandori and Nicoletti stopped to allow their eyes to adjust. From the far end of the barn, they heard voices and the sound of furniture being dragged across a wooden floor.

At the back of the barn was a tack room separated from the main building by half walls and topped with small-paned glass windows. In the center of the room was a desk and several wooden chairs. On the back wall were dozens of nylon horse leads, several saddles, and shelves of tools and hanging bridles. A narrow hallway led to a room with more tack and horse blankets where the suspect slept.

Tim Benson stood in the corner of the small room, watching the officers sift through his belongings. Chief Garland stood next to him, leaning on the wall and chewing on a piece of straw. Garland nodded as Pandori and Nicoletti entered.

"Take a look at this," one of the uniformed officers called to Reichert and held up a stack of magazines he had pulled from under a pile of clothes on the floor of the closet.

Pandori and Reichert moved toward the officer.

Garland pushed Tim Benson into a chair. "Stay there until Detective Reichert tells you to move," Garland said. "Mike, I'm going outside for a minute," he said to Reichert. As he passed Nicoletti, he spit the straw on the floor and said, "Come with me."

Garland took a beige cowboy hat from his car and set it on the back of his head.

"What do you think?" he asked Nicoletti.

"Anything is possible, but I think he's much too young. Marie-Justine's killer has been at this for a while.

The hair, the makeup, the red choker are all preferences developed over years, maybe over decades. If you can tie Benson to an older, more mature suspect, someone with a history of violence, then it's an outside possibility. But acting alone? No way, Chief. Benson is too young."

"I don't know about him being too young, but I agree he didn't do it."

"What about the prior arrest for rape?"

"That was a bullshit charge. And I should know; I was the one who arrested him. It was my case."

Garland pulled the hat forward on his head and put on a pair of sunglasses. He put his hands in his pockets and walked to the paddock area with Nicoletti at his side.

"You have any idea what it's like growing up as a local, or worse, as a country boy in a university town?" He looked at Nicoletti from under the brim of his hat.

"Can't say I do."

"Every day you're surrounded with pretty girls walking in town, sitting in cafés, driving past you in their fancy cars. They seem to be part of a different world."

Nicoletti nodded as he looked across the gentle hills. Three horses were grazing in the shade of a stand of trees. The leaves were a vibrant green and yellow with a touch of red against the dark blue sky.

Leaning on the white paddock fence, Garland rested a tan boot on the lowest crossbar. "And you know, they really are from a different world. They come from all over the country, from big cities that could swallow up Missoula so you could never find it again." He pushed his hat back. "Once in a while, one of those girls actually dates a local boy. Not often, but it has happened. Every lonely high school kid secretly fantasizes that one day a pretty coed from New York or California is going to stop and talk to him. Maybe talk long enough to fall in love with him. Sounds pretty silly, doesn't it?"

"What's that got to do with the rape charge?" Nicoletti continued to watch the horses.

"The complainant in the case, a twenty-year-old sophomore from Boston, claimed that she met Benson at a concert. They had a few beers, she got drunk, and he offered to take her back to her apartment. She said she passed out on the couch, and when she came to, she was naked in her bed and he was forcing himself on her. She said she had begged him to stop and tried to fight him off, but couldn't."

"Doesn't sound too farfetched."

"The victim had a roommate who identified Benson. She said she had been out with friends and got back to the apartment around midnight. Benson and the victim were on the couch, drinking wine. She said hello to them and noticed that the victim was pretty drunk. She had suggested that Benson leave, but he ignored her.

"She said she left them on the couch, showered, and went to bed. Claimed she didn't hear anything; said she had taken a sleeping pill that knocked her out. When she got up about eleven Sunday morning, her roommate and Benson were gone.

"The victim didn't report the assault until Sunday afternoon. She showed up at the station with her boyfriend and the roommate."

"Let me guess… By then, she had cleaned up, so there was no physical evidence?"

"No, we got some of Benson's hair—long blond strands caught up in a rubber band I found on the victim's bedroom floor. He had used the rubber band to tie his hair in a ponytail. And there were a couple of used condoms in the trash."

"Thoughtful rapist."

"Actually, it was more accurately a prepared victim. Only her prints were on the foil wrappers, and the remains of a box of twelve were found in her dresser drawer under some thong panties."

"Did you say a couple of condoms?"

"There were three."

"All matching the Benson kid's DNA?"

"We never got that far."

"Why the delay in reporting the assault?"

"The victim and her boyfriend had gone to church Sunday morning, then to lunch. When they got back to the apartment, Benson was sitting on the front steps. He walked up to the victim and said, 'I thought we were going riding this afternoon' and walked away without another word. According to the roommate, he had been to the apartment earlier, looking for the victim, and had left a bouquet of flowers for her."

"Not typical rapist behavior, unless the perp is a real psycho," Nicoletti said. "Where was the boyfriend on Saturday night?"

"He had broken up with the alleged victim a few days before. He said he wanted to date other people."

"So maybe Miss Boston took on the Benson kid to make the boyfriend jealous."

"That's what I figured. She probably would have never discussed the incident with anyone, but with Benson waiting on the front steps and acting like a jilted lover, followed by the flowers on the dining room table in the apartment, she probably felt compelled to come up with a story for the boyfriend."

"And 'he raped me' was the best she could do?"

"Buyer's remorse," Garland said. "Monday morning, an assistant DA insisted on filing the complaint before I had a chance to get Benson's version of the story."

"Why was the assistant in such a rush?"

"All sex is rape," Garland said. "You know the type."

"What did Benson say after you picked him up?"

"For the most part, he corroborated the victim's account of the first half of the evening. He said she had invited him to her apartment. They opened a bottle of wine and were making out when the roommate came in. The three of them talked for a while and had planned to go riding out here at the ranch the next afternoon. Then they all went to bed."

"Together?"

"No, but if half of what Benson said really happened, I'm sure by Sunday morning, he thought he was in love."

"So what happened to the case?" Nicoletti asked.

"The roommate was the first to break. She didn't have the stomach to ruin the kid's life. In her second version, there was no sleeping pill. In fact, she said she was up half the night listening to the laughter and moaning coming from the next room. She said at about four A.M. she could smell popcorn cooking. I found popcorn in the bed, and in the bedroom trash can, there was a crumpled bag of microwave popcorn with a condom draped across Orville Redenbacher's face."

"Classic," Nicoletti said.

"When I confronted the victim with the roommate's statement, she denied it and insisted the sex was not consensual. According to her, I was an incompetent bastard who was trying to protect another low-rent, ignorant redneck cowboy." Garland took off his hat and wiped his brow. "But in the end, she refused to cooperate with the assistant DA, and she and the boyfriend transferred to some college back East."

"Why are you telling this story to me?" Nicoletti looked directly at Garland.

"I don't know. While I was in the barn, standing with Benson, I realized that I'd forgotten what this job is all about. The last year, I've been totally focused on politics and running for sheriff."

Nicoletti turned his gaze to the horses and said nothing.

"Since Marie-Justine was murdered, I've been in meeting after meeting with the DA and the mayor and on the phone with the state attorney general. All we've discussed was the impact of this type of crime on the election. The only interest any of us had in catching the killer was directly related to our own ambitions."

Garland reached in his jacket pocket and took out a plastic bag of marijuana.

"What do you think?" He held up the bag. "About an ounce?"

"I guess that's about right." Nicoletti took the bag. "Where'd you get it?"

"Benson pulled it out from under his mattress and gave it to me before the others got here."

"What are you going to do with it?"

"You're the retired DEA agent. You tell me."

Nicoletti took the bag and shook the contents into the wind. "The kid's got enough trouble. And I'm not running for sheriff." Nicoletti handed him the empty bag.

"Neither am I," Garland said.

FIFTY-NINE

Nicoletti was standing in Anne Bertone's kitchen when his cell phone rang. Ken Palmer was calling from Colorado Springs with something solid to report.

"On that trespassing conviction, there wasn't much on Charles Durbin other than he pled no contest to the charge," Palmer began. "But I was able to run down some information that might be of interest."

Nicoletti waited.

"I talked to a retired Colorado state trooper who used to work for me in the task force. He runs a private investigative service here in the Springs. Last year, he was hired by a local law firm to keep an eye on a wealthy, young divorcee living in one of those mansions over in the Broadmoor area. Seems that the woman believed she was being followed and her lawyers wanted to make sure it wasn't the ex-husband, who, they say, got burned pretty badly in the settlement. You got me so far?"

"I'm just retired, not deaf," Nicoletti said.

"Anyway, the trooper is following her around town, keeping an eye on the house—you know, the usual. About a week goes by and he doesn't spot anything. Then one night, the woman, who my guy said is a knock-out, decides to go for a little nighttime skinny-dip in her indoor pool, the kind that's enclosed in one of those glass conservatory-type additions. You know?"

"Yeah, I know. Go on already. Are you trying to piss me off?"

"Yeah."

"Well, it's working."

"So the trooper is clocking a little overtime, standing in the far corner of the yard, straining his eyes to get a better look through the steamed-over glass, when he catches a shadow moving between him and the building. He watches as this guy, who turns out to be your guy, Durbin, steps up to the window and starts walking back and forth, keeping up with the woman as she swims laps.

"Now, get this, the trooper said he thinks the guy was playing with himself while he's peeping at Lady Godiva doing the backstroke."

Palmer paused, but did not wait for a response.

"He tries to move in on the peeper, but the guy hears him and makes a beeline for the garden wall. The trooper catches him as he's going over the top and pulls him down. He said Durbin started to put up one hell of a fight, but after a little pepper spray and a thump with a blackjack, Durbin folds into the fetal position and begins to cry, yelling, 'Don't hurt me. I'm sorry.' So the trooper cuffs him up and calls in the Springs PD to haul him off." Palmer waited a beat. "What do you think of that?"

"Very interesting," Nicoletti said slowly.

"Yeah, very interesting. So I asked if they ever figured out how this Durbin got fixated on the swimmer. The trooper tells me that she identified him as a hair stylist working at the Broadmoor Hotel, where she gets her hair done."

"I know you've got more," Nicoletti said.

"Yeah, I went to the hotel and talked to the salon manager. She says Durbin was terminated right before the incident. They had two complaints that he followed female guests to their rooms and tried to strike up conversations with them in the hall.

"You know the Broadmoor; they're not going to put up with that kind of crap. I'm surprised they waited for the second complaint. So the manager lets me take a look at his job application in his personnel folder. He didn't list any family members, all the contact numbers were local, and he previously worked for a hair joint in Chicago that supplied him with a letter of reference. I followed up with his landlady, and it looks like he moved out right after he settled the court case. They charged him with trespassing. No forwarding address… Oh, and the court gave him a suspended sentence. It was his first offense."

"I have something else I need you to do," Nicoletti said. "Check with the surrounding jurisdictions and see if there are any unsolved homicides of females—let's say early twenties to late forties—who were strangled by ligature during the time Durbin lived in the Colorado Springs area."

"You think this Durbin graduated from Peeping Tom to the Boston strangler?" Palmer sounded like he was taking notes.

"If you find any open cases, get a look at the file and check to see if the victims had their hair combed in an unusual style or were wearing excessive makeup that wouldn't have been normal for them." Nicoletti struggled to complete his thought without the crime scene photos of Marie-Justine appearing before him. "I also need to know if the bodies were missing any articles of clothing when they were found, like underwear, and check to see if there is any evidence of penetration, particularly, the lack of it."

"So you're thinking Durbin is a stalking souvenir collector who can't get it up?"

"Whatever. Call me when you get anything close."

"Hey, Nico... How about 'thanks, Ken' or 'good job, Ken'?"

"Thanks, Ken. Good job, Ken," Nicoletti said flatly. "You know, Palmer, you never struck me as one of those sensitive types who need positive feedback."

"It's the stress of retirement, Nico. I just need to feel appreciated again."

SIXTY

The last of the afternoon sun washed across Anne's living room wall. Nicoletti sat in an overstuffed chair, sipping a glass of red wine. Anne had gone into her bedroom after he briefed her on Ken Palmer's call. Nicoletti reviewed his options as he swirled the wine, absently inspecting its color and bouquet.

Pandori called to remind Nicoletti that he was going to Billings the following morning to review the files of the two unsolved murders. He offered to delay his trip if Nicoletti wanted him to stay in Missoula. Nicoletti declined. He was relieved Pandori would be out of town. He had a plan and believed it would be better if Pandori was far away with a valid alibi.

Anne crossed the fading lines of sunlight in a low-cut black dress that followed the athletic curves of her body to just above her knees. She held a bottle of perfume in front of her, creating misty clouds that she walked through on her way to Nicoletti's side.

"I've thought it over, and tonight, as long as Reichert and Pandori have everything under control, I'm going to let you take me out to dinner," she said.

"Don't you think—"

"Stop." She held the perfume bottle like a talisman to ward off evil spirits. "We're going to your hotel. You are going to clean up and put on some nice clothes, and we are going out. If anything happens, the guys will call you on your cell. But until then, we are going to dinner like two civilized people who aren't consumed and confused with some sort of insane—"

"What is that perfume?" The scent brought a flood of Marie-Justine's images and emotions to his consciousness.

"It's Jivago." She turned to look at him. "I gave a bottle of it to M-J last Saturday. It's our favorite. Come in here and I'll show you the holder it sits in. M-J just thought it was the coolest thing." She entered the bedroom.

Nicoletti pulled himself up from the chair. Anne's change in mood took him by surprise. He had been thinking about Marie-Justine also, but not about her perfume. He had been thinking of ways to avenge her death.

SIXTY-ONE

From the front window, Durbin watched the patrol car slow down as it passed his house for the second time. The side of the vehicle displayed the sheriff's department emblem. He was accustomed to seeing the Missoula police occasionally roll down the street but could not remember ever seeing a sheriff's vehicle in the neighborhood.

He went into the kitchen, turned on the faucet, and waited for the water to cool before filling a glass. Through the window above the sink, he could see the line of privacy fences that separated his neighbors' gardens and backyards from the dusty alley that ran behind the properties.

Durbin had thought of replacing the low chain link fence behind his house with a six-foot wooden privacy fence to match the neighbors', but he had never gotten around to it. To put in the fence now would be foolish. He was not going to be around long enough to enjoy it. "Let the next owner make the improvement," he said, raising the water glass in a toast to his planned departure from Missoula.

Over the top of the fences he saw the red-and-blue light bar of the sheriff's car moving down the alley. He went to the windows at the back of the house and leaned over the washer and dryer, pushing the curtains to the side. The sheriff's patrol car stopped behind the house, next to the gray Suburban. Durbin glanced at the back door. It was locked, the deadbolt and security chain in place. He looked out the window again. The patrol car moved down the alley. He unlocked the back door and walked across the tiny backyard. Over the gate of the chain link fence, he looked down the alley. The patrol car was gone.

Someone was knocking on the front door when he set the water glass in the sink. Gradually, the knocking became more forceful.

"Good afternoon. I'm Deputy Glick from the sheriff's office. Are you Charles Durbin?"

"Yes. Can I help you?"

"I'm conducting a follow-up investigation and I'd like to ask you a few questions." The deputy held up a thin manila file folder as if to indicate that the questions were contained within.

"Sure. An investigation about what?" Durbin started to step outside and pull the door closed behind him, but the deputy moved forward, blocking his path.

"It will only take a few minutes. I'll just come in and we can get started."

"We can talk out here. I'm just about—"

Deputy Glick pushed past Durbin and entered the house. Durbin closed the door and followed the uninvited guest to the kitchen.

"Can I get you something to drink?"

"No, thank you."

"So, what is it I can help you with?" Durbin turned his back on the deputy and took the glass from the sink. "Are you sure you wouldn't like some water?"

"There was a crime committed near the university Sunday night." Glick ignored the offer of hospitality and sat at the kitchen table. "We're checking on vehicles that match the description of those reported to have been in the area."

"What type of crime?"

"It was a homicide."

"Homicide. How horrible." Durbin affected his speech and held his free hand to his chest in an effort to appear slightly effeminate. He evaluated the deputy, who was looking down as he shuffled through the paperwork in the file. He was a large man made larger by the bullet-proof vest beneath his tan uniform shirt. Durbin was a little disappointed that the deputy had not observed his theatrical gesture. "Who was killed?"

"A woman, a professor at the university, named Cantrell. Did you know her?" The deputy looked up.

"I read in the paper she was killed near the river." Durbin took a drink, hiding his face behind the glass.

"She was. But she lived a few blocks from the university." The deputy waited for Durbin to lower the glass. "Did you know her?"

"No, thank God. How terrible to have someone you love murdered."

"Someone you love?" Deputy Glick stared at Durbin.

Durbin could feel the blood rush into his face. "I mean... her poor family... such a tragedy... so awful for them."

"Yeah, I'm sure." The deputy pulled a pen from his shirt pocket. "So last Sunday night, where were you between about ten and midnight?"

"I don't know. Home, I guess." He took another drink, then refilled his glass. "Did someone say they saw my car over there?"

"No. We've just got some general descriptions of the types of vehicles seen in the area that didn't belong there." The deputy waited for Durbin to turn from the sink. "Your Suburban matches the description of one of the vehicles."

"I remember…" Durbin dragged the word out as if being called back from a dream. "I was parked over there last Sunday night. I had gone over to the university to run on the track."

"That late at night?" The deputy made some notes.

"I often run late at night. It's cooler."

"Why did you park so far away from the track? Why not use the parking lot that's right next to it?"

"I usually park a few blocks away. It gives me a chance to warm up before I run and cool down before I get back into the car." Durbin became comfortable with his answers. He put down the glass. His confidence was growing. He noticed that the deputy was large but soft. *No match for my strength and endurance,* Durbin thought.

"What was that?" Deputy Glick asked. "Did you just say something?"

"No." Durbin sat next to him. "Is there anything else?"

"Did you go running alone?"

"Yes, I always run alone. I'm training for the Missoula marathon next spring and I find it difficult to set my pace when I run with someone."

"Was there anyone who saw you on the track that night?"

"No." Durbin thought he answered too quickly, too definitely. "I don't think so." That sounded better. "I did pass someone on the street as I walked from my car. A woman with a small dog, a brown-and-white terrier, but I didn't speak to her. Actually, I really didn't get a good look at her. It was dark and she had a hat on. I think she was wearing glasses." Durbin stopped. That was enough. He didn't want to give too much information. He had read somewhere that liars are often too specific.

"Do you keep a diary?"

"A diary?" What kind of question was that?

"Yeah, my partner trained for the marathon last year and he kept a diary—you know, training days, distance, times, that sort of diary. He even kept track of what he ate each day."

"Oh, a training diary. Sure." Durbin felt nervous. The conversation was getting too far into a subject he had just invented.

Deputy Glick put his hand on the blue-and-white tablecloth and inspected the matching Provençal-style placemats. He looked at the delicate teacup and saucer on the other side of the table. "Are you married, Mr. Durbin?"

"No."

"Have a girlfriend?"

"No. I've been looking, but—"

"How about we go out back and take a look at your car?" Deputy Glick let go of the placemat and stood up, closed the folder, and put the pen in his pocket.

Durbin led the way. He could feel the deputy behind him, expecting at any second to be grabbed by the shoulders, slammed to the ground, and handcuffed.

The deputy walked slowly around the Suburban. When he came to the driver's door, he reached for the handle and pulled it open.

"Mind if I look inside?" He placed the manila folder on the seat.

Durbin saw the edge of the green nylon bag showing from under the driver's seat. He wanted to pull the deputy away from the car and slam the door.

"No, go ahead," he bluffed. "What are you looking for?"

"Don't exactly know." The deputy leaned into the car. "My wife has been begging me to get rid of our truck and buy one of these. What kind of mileage do you get?" He shifted to block Durbin's view as he opened the center console.

"About fourteen miles to the gallon."

Deputy Glick faced him, holding the knife in the brown leather sheath. Durbin started to reach to grab the knife but stopped his left hand before it betrayed his panic.

"You been in the military, Mr. Durbin?" Glick studied the ribbon attached to the sheath. He pulled the knife out far enough to expose the engraving on the blade. He looked hard at Durbin.

"That was a gift from a neighbor of mine."

"One of your neighbors here?"

"No… in Colorado… near Fort Carson. That's just south of Colorado Springs."

"I know where Fort Carson is. Seems like the kind of thing a soldier would give to his son or grandson." The deputy slid the knife back into the sheath.

"He only had a daughter, and she made it pretty clear she hated anything that had to do with the army."

"Well, it's a real collector's item." He handed the knife to Durbin. "I wouldn't leave it out here in an unlocked car." He reached in, closed the console, and picked up the file folder.

The deputy closed the car door and stepped toward Durbin. This time, Durbin did not retreat. He felt the weight of the knife in his hand and imagined moving into the deputy and driving the blade up through his neck into his brain.

"Is that it?" Durbin asked.

"For now." Deputy Glick moved past Durbin and headed back into the house. "If there is anything else, someone will be in touch."

Durbin set the knife on the kitchen table. The deputy was already out the front door.

"Thanks for your cooperation, Mr. Durbin."

"Glad I could help," Durbin said as he closed the door. "My time here is running out."

SIXTY-TWO

Deputy Glick pulled into a gas station on Main Street. He took the manila folder and walked over to another sheriff's vehicle parked at the edge of the station in the shade of a large tree.

"How'd you make out?" The sergeant asked Glick.

"I got through about half the vehicles on my list. Only two were the right color: one belonged to an elderly couple who never go out at night, and the other to a guy who runs a dog grooming shop. He admitted he was parked in the area of the victim's home on Saturday night but said he was jogging over at the university. He's some kind of runner. Think he's half a fag."

"The other guys struck out too."

"This is bullshit, Sarge. What's the point? We spend all day driving around looking for a Suburban—gray, silver, maybe light green, or whatever—while that fucking Reichert sits at his desk, dreaming up some other crap for us to do."

"It's got to be done, Glick."

"Why? Because some old lady, who probably doesn't know a Suburban from a Cadillac, said she saw one driving up and down her street the night of the murder?" He took the folder from under his arm and shook it. "If locating this car is so important, why don't the police do it?"

"The Sheriff wants us to help. So whatever they need us to do, we're going to do it."

"Well, I'm done for the day. My kid has a soccer game over at the middle school and I promised him I'd be there." He handed the folder to the sergeant. "Turn this in for me. I'll get to the rest of the list after my days off."

"This may be over before then." the sergeant said, placing the folder on the front seat of the patrol car. "I got a call from Reichert saying they got a tip on a graduate student who had been stalking Professor Cantrell. They're headed over to interview him now."

"Good. The sooner this is over, the better. These last few days, my wife has been spending most of her time locking windows and doors. Then she walks around, checking to make sure they're locked. The rest of her time she spends calling me on my cell to ask if I'm in the neighborhood and when I'm coming home." Deputy Glick got back into his car and looked at the sergeant. "You know, there's something about that Durbin guy that's just not right."

"Like what?"

"I don't know. He's just not right." Deputy Glick drove off.

The sergeant opened the folder. At the top of the page, he wrote: *Charles Durbin—follow-up interview needed.*

SIXTY-THREE

Detective Reichert stood in the center of Perry Sommer's living room. Sommer sat on the couch. Two campus police officers in dark blue uniforms stood behind Reichert.

"So let me get this straight," Reichert said. "You're a graduate student, working as a teaching assistant for Dr. Kimba?"

"Was… was working for Dr. Kimba," Sommer corrected. He looked toward the campus police officers for approval.

"On the night Dr. Kimba died," Reichert continued, "you met with him at his office?"

"That's correct."

"What was the meeting for?"

"To discuss some of the students who were having problems in one of his classes." Sommer leaned forward and rested his elbows on his knees.

"Did Dr. Kimba seem worried about anything? Was he distracted or seem preoccupied?"

"No more than usual. Dr. Kimba was brilliant. His mind was always pondering several things at once. Sometimes we would meet to discuss an issue and never get around to addressing it."

"And that night, did he stay on topic?"

"Yes. As a matter of fact, he was quite on point. He was in a rush, said he had another meeting. He gave me a stack of review notes and told me to organize a special session with the students to go over them."

"Did he say who he was meeting?"

"No."

"Then what?"

"Then I left."

"Did Dr. Kimba leave at the same time?"

"No. He left a few minutes later. I saw him walking across campus toward his house."

"Had you ever been to his house?"

"Yes, several times."

Lenny Pandori came into the living room from Sommer's bedroom. He handed Reichert ten photographs. Reichert looked through the photos and turned to Sommer.

"Did you know Professor Marie-Justine Cantrell?" Reichert asked.

"Not really." Sommer folded his arms across his chest.

Pandori sat down close to Sommer, who shifted toward the corner of the couch. Reichert waited.

"She was a friend of Dr. Kimba's," Sommer finally said. "He introduced us. I've seen her around." Sommer waited for the next question, but the two investigators said nothing. "I talked to her a few times." Sommer crossed his legs and looked at the floor. "She was a very nice person."

"When did you take these pictures of her?" Reichert held out the photographs and waved them in front of Sommer.

"Over the last couple of months. I take a lot of pictures."

Pandori moved closer to Sommer. "Why were the pictures of Professor Cantrell separated from the others in your closet?"

"After I heard she was killed, I pulled them out." Sommer tried to move away from Pandori, but there was no room.

Reichert shuffled through the photographs. Marie-Justine Cantrell was frozen in time, going about her life in different parts of town, wearing different outfits, smiling, talking to people, sitting at an outdoor café.

"Do you know Anne Bertone?" Reichert asked. "She's in several of these pictures." He showed a photo to Sommer and pointed to Anne.

"No. She's just a friend of Dr. Cantrell's, I guess. I've seen them around town together."

"Some of these pictures have been cropped. Did you develop and print them yourself?"

"Sure, at the art building photo lab."

"Do you have the original negatives?" Reichert asked.

"I keep all my negatives in a box in the bedroom closet."

"Get up and get me all the negatives and any other pictures you have of Dr. Cantrell," Reichert ordered.

Sommer hesitated, his arms and legs crossed. "I don't know if that's legal. Is it?" Sommer directed his question to the campus officers.

Reichert turned to the uniformed officers. "Please wait in the hall," he said.

The officers complied, shutting Sommer's apartment door behind them.

Before Sommer could voice any objection, Reichert was on top of him, pinning his legs against the couch. Pandori grabbed Sommer's folded arms and trapped them against the student's chest.

Reichert leaned his left hand hard against Sommer's throat. "Now, get up and get me those fucking pictures and negatives, you smart-ass piece of shit."

SIXTY-FOUR

At nine thirty the next morning, Nicoletti was sitting in the rental car, watching the rear of Durbin's house. Anne was parked across the road, with a view of the street in front and the alley behind.

He would have preferred to have Reichert and Pandori assisting him, but this phase of his plan had to be implemented with as few witnesses as possible. Besides, Nicoletti believed that Pandori and Reichert would seriously jeopardize their careers by participating.

Anne agreed to act as a lookout, and Nicoletti convinced himself that she was all the help he needed. Besides, it was all the help he had.

Nicoletti observed movement at the back of the house. He dialed Anne's cell phone and told her to expect Durbin's Suburban to exit the alley. She stayed on the line and soon reported that the Suburban was traveling away from the residence and confirmed that Durbin was the lone occupant.

Anne had arranged for an elderly friend to make a ten o'clock appointment with Durbin to come to her home to groom her four-year-old Saint Bernard.

Nicoletti checked his watch; it was fifteen minutes before ten. Based on Anne's description of the one-hundred-and-fifty-pound dog, Nicoletti figured he had at least one hour to spend in the house before he needed to worry about Durbin's return.

The deadbolt on the back door was an obstacle beyond Nicoletti's lock-picking capabilities. The time he wasted on the back door and his fruitless search for an open window had eaten up fifteen precious minutes. Fortunately, a side door yielded to the unsophisticated pressure of Nicoletti's left shoulder.

Carried by his momentum, he found himself hanging on to the fragile wooden door, trying to maintain his balance at the top of a flight of narrow stone steps leading to the dark bowels of the house. Regaining his footing, he closed the door behind him, sealing out any hint of light.

He fumbled in a fanny pack he had borrowed from Anne until he found the small flashlight he had purchased at the local hardware store earlier that morning. Even with fresh batteries, the light was minimal, providing a weak yellow glow that only served to enhance the eerie quality of the earthen walls and dusty stone floor.

He crossed the basement, slowly making his way to a set of wooden stairs that led up into the house. He noted two large trunks and a suitcase surrounded by a number of cardboard moving boxes. He would inspect their contents later, if time allowed.

At the top of the wooden stairs was a door held closed by a hook and eye. Nicoletti again searched the fanny pack. The hook was loose enough to allow the blade of a screwdriver to spring it free.

Nicoletti stepped from the darkness into the light of Durbin's kitchen, only it wasn't Durbin's at all—it was Marie-Justine's kitchen that greeted him. Nicoletti moved slowly from table to counter to window. The furnishings, tablecloth, glassware, appliances, and curtains were, to the best of his recollection, identical to those in the little yellow-and-white cottage.

Stalled with a mix of confusion and revulsion, Nicoletti forced himself out of the kitchen. He glanced at the grooming area before entering into the sparsely furnished parlor. Through an archway, he found himself back in the kitchen. To his left were the laundry room and the bolted back door. He looked at his watch, then at the back door through which he could anticipate Durbin's return in less than thirty minutes.

He climbed the stairs, testing each tread to avoid excessive creaking. Each step was solid and his assent was silent. The staircase led to a circular landing on the second floor. Nicoletti paused, looking at three doors, all of them closed.

He waited another moment. Holding his breath, he strained to hear if there were any sounds of life coming from behind the three closed doors. Confident in his isolation, he walked toward the front of the house and opened the door on his left.

Slowly, he moved through the doorway. From the contents, he assumed that it was Durbin's bedroom. Every item in the room was meticulously set in place, giving the appearance that the room was preserved in a museum, not subject to the daily stresses and strains of being occupied. The room was so pristine that Nicoletti stepped only on the parts of the wooden floor not covered by the area rugs, which appeared freshly vacuumed and ready to preserve the memory of any intruder's footprint.

Before inspecting the contents of the dresser, he examined it to see if the drawers had been set with calibrated openings of a fraction of an inch or left with small trigger devices—a hair, a piece of paper, or a match—that would fall to the ground, unnoticed by an intruder. Nothing caught his eye.

In keeping with the décor of the room, the interiors of the drawers were organized in such a regimented fashion that Nicoletti decided not to touch any of their contents.

He opened the closet and found no hidden storage compartments. A wooden panel in the closet ceiling showed no signs of use, no scrapes or markings to indicate frequent access to items stored above its small opening. He nodded a silent greeting to the gray coat that was hanging among the well-ordered garments— the coat he was sure had covered the arm whose hand touched Marie-Justine's hair on Saturday morning.

The drawers of the nightstands that flanked the neatly made double bed were empty. At each corner of the bed was a massive wooden post. The posts were carved and slightly tapered but still three inches thick at the top. He tried to twist the tops of the four bedposts to see if they unscrewed. They did not.

He moved the framed photographs of rock formations that adorned the walls but found nothing hidden behind them.

In a narrow alcove between the bedroom and the bath was a linen closet. Nicoletti pulled the stacks of perfectly folded towels out, but again found nothing. From the alcove, he dropped to a push-up position and looked across the floor under the bed. The only thing that caught his eye was the slight impression of the edge of his own footprint sketched in a chalk-like dust on the polished wooden floor.

He examined the black rubber soles of his boots and felt the rise of panic in his chest. How many footprints had he made? Where were they? The dust must have come from the cellar stairs.

He reached in the linen closet and removed a hand towel. He wiped the boots, then the bedroom floor. The hall and staircase he could get on his way out.

Fifteen minutes left.

He stuffed the towel into the fanny pack. If Durbin counted towels at the end of every day, he would certainly have something to keep him awake tonight, Nicoletti thought.

The medicine cabinet was as organized as the dresser. Several plastic vials of prescription medication were on the lower shelf. Nicoletti wondered which of the colorful pills were to be used to diminish Durbin's compulsive behavior and which controlled his homicidal fantasies. He opened the door behind him. It opened onto the circular landing, a few feet from the top of the stairs.

Nicoletti crossed the landing and opened the last of the three doors. It was another bedroom that also appeared to be unoccupied. The shades were drawn. He turned on the light. The room seemed familiar. Then he focused on the plaster wall behind the bed. It was Anne's bedroom, replicated right down to the rocking chair near the window, the position of the dresser, the rug, the nightstand, and the lamps. Nicoletti opened the nightstand drawer. Good, he thought. No gun.

As he turned from the bedside, he saw the painting. It was of a woman, a beautiful woman, with dark hair and large green eyes. Her hair was combed to the side and held with a silver comb. Her lips were red and full. A red choker was painted around her neck—not painted by the artist but added crudely by someone else. The seductive energy of the painting repelled him as he recalled the crime scene photos of Marie-Justine.

He stumbled backward, catching himself on the edge of the dresser. He turned in time to catch a slender cut glass bottle as it started to tip from the impact of his weight against the furniture. He held it for a moment and recognized the shape. Then he placed the tapered bottle back in its clouded glass holder.

He heard Anne's voice inside his head: *M-J just thought it was the coolest thing.* It was a bottle of Jivago perfume. He pictured Anne handing the perfume to Marie-Justine at the café. *I wanted to give you something*, she had said.

Inside the top drawer of the dresser, he found what he had been looking for: souvenirs, or trophies, from Durbin's adventures. On the right were several pairs of women's underwear, some worn, some new. On the left were five locks of hair, each bound with waxed thread. He picked up the lock of chestnut hair, held it for a moment, then gently returned it to its resting place. He closed the drawer.

Between the dresser and the wall, he noticed the corner of a canvas stretched on a wooden frame. He pulled it out and turned it toward the light coming from the hall.

It was a painting of a nude woman, kneeling as if in prayer, in a dense forest. A shaft of light passed through the foliage and illuminated the woman's blond hair and the top of her left shoulder. Nicoletti returned the canvas to its hiding place.

He straightened the rug and turned out the light. As he closed the door, he saw the rocking chair and thought for a moment of sitting in it and waiting for Durbin to walk into his trophy room.

The cell phone rang. It was Anne.

"He's coming back." Panic was in her voice.

"We're okay. I'm all done."

"No. He's coming back down the alley."

"I thought your friend was supposed to call you when he left her house," he said quickly, surveying the upstairs hall, then bounding down the stairs.

"She did. She just called. Then, before I could call you, he was here."

Nicoletti shut off the phone. He raced through the grooming area and the kitchen to the back door. He heard the sound of the Suburban's tires on the gravel drive behind the house. He retraced his steps back into the kitchen, closed the basement door, and hooked it shut.

Once outside, he turned on his cell phone and called Anne. "Everything is okay. I'm out."

"Jesus, Nicoletti. Now what?"

"Meet me at Justine's."

SIXTY-FIVE

Nicoletti walked directly into Marie-Justine's bedroom. He scanned the top of the dressing table. The new bottle of Jivago was not there. Anne looked in the bathroom and in a few other places as he described to her what he had seen in Durbin's home. Convinced the perfume was not to be found, they stopped their search and stood at the foot of the bed.

Nicoletti's cell phone rang. Anne jumped, still unsettled by the thought of her own bedroom having an identical twin across town. Nicoletti had not told her about the neatly arranged bundles of hair or the women's underwear he had found in Durbin's guest room. Anne would demand they go to the police, and that was something Nicoletti did not intend to do, at least not yet.

The cell phone rang a second time.

"I found two," Ken Palmer said.

"Two?"

"Yeah, two unsolved homicides of women. The first was a Realtor, late thirties, wealthy, very good-looking.

Her husband reported her missing when she didn't show up for a dinner party. Her car, a gold Lexus, was found two days later in the parking lot of a hotel on the north end of the Springs.

"The body was found about two months later in a wooded area near a rest stop on Interstate 25, about ten miles north. Heavy snow had covered the body, so there was minimal decomposition, minor animal damage."

"Were there any suspects?"

"Getting to that," Palmer said. "Seems the police focused on the husband, a local home builder with major bucks. She was cheating on him and the marriage was in the toilet. She had multiple lovers, all from the most prestigious country clubs, most of them married. I bet the damn investigation caused one hell of a social shitstorm.

"Anyway, the investigation was on the front burner as the cops chased the husband and the boyfriends for about six months. There were a hundred other leads, mostly coming from acquaintances and co-workers— you know, the usual kind of stuff that's generated by petty jealousies. With her money, good looks, and success, I bet they were lining up to share their dirty little rumors. Nothing came of any of it and pretty soon the leads dried up completely."

"Anything in the files tie her to Durbin?"

"Now, don't get too far out ahead of me, old buddy. I found a copy of her day planner that the cops had in a cardboard box in the basement of the PD. It showed that she scheduled regular hair appointments at the Broadmoor Hotel during the time your little creep worked there."

Nicoletti realized he was alone in the bedroom. He found Anne seated at the kitchen table. She was pale and appeared startled by the sound of his voice.

"What about physical evidence?"

"Nothing recovered at the dump site or from the victim's car."

"Manner of death?" Nicoletti could hear Palmer flipping through pages of notes.

"Strangulation by ligature, which was described as approximately one-half-inch wide and about one-eighth inch thick, probably woven nylon. Her skin was pinched at the back of her neck. No marks other than scratches on her neck, which were attributed to her own nails as she tried to pull at the ligature.

"No indication of rape. No DNA recovered. I couldn't tell from the crime scene photos if she had any excessive makeup like you were looking for. Her hair was a mess, but in the evidence, I did find one of those plastic hair combs that could have been used to pull her hair to the side. It was spray-painted silver, but the paint was flaking off. And before you ask, yeah, the panties were missing from the recovered body."

"What was the other one? You said 'two'." Nicoletti sat across from Anne. She did not look at him.

"The second one occurred a month after the Realtor disappeared. This one was younger, twenty-three. She lived north of the Springs in El Paso County. Her body was found in a mountainous area where a lot of high school kids go camping, which is a local euphemism for drinking and smoking dope. She had short dark hair, but otherwise was similar to the woman in the swimming pool I told you about: five foot six, long legs, tiny waist, full breasted, pretty face, full lips. Her father was a light colonel assigned to Fort Carson here in the Springs.

"Sheriff's investigators said the old man took it really hard. She was his only child, a tomboy but still Daddy's little girl, I guess." Palmer hesitated.

Nicoletti was sure both he and Palmer were thinking of their own daughters.

"She was a part-time singer… no steady boy-friends," Palmer continued. "She associated mostly with musicians… kept a lot of late nights… often gone two or three days at a time without telling anyone. If the killer hadn't dumped her near that camping area, no telling how long it would have been before someone noticed she was missing."

"How was she killed?"

"Strangulation. Manual. Killer wore gloves. None of that makeup shit or hair combing like the others. This girl was beat pretty bad. Her face was bloody and she had bruises on her arms and knuckles. Deputies said she must've put up one hell of a fight. There were blood samples recovered that did not match the victim, but there were no DNA matches in the system.

"They did find a head wound. The coroner said she was hit with a blunt object, rounded at the top and tapered toward the base. There was an impression of stitching at the edge of the wound. They guessed it was some type of lead-weighted blackjack or sap—you know, like we used to carry, kind of spring-loaded with the braided leather strap. No bigger than your thumb, but if you snap it just right, you can split a guy's head open like a melon."

"Did she have any connection to the Broadmoor?"

"No, none that I could find. I didn't ask."

"It sure as hell would help."

"Well, it ain't a perfect world, Nico." Palmer sounded like he was about done. "Oh yeah, on the body, they found fibers matching her carpet and some cat hair that matched her cat."

"She had a cat?" Nicoletti stood up.

"Yeah, one of those Siamese type cats. There was a picture of it in the victim's wallet."

"Palmer, I want you to find every veterinarian and pet groomer she ever took that cat to. And then check to see if Durbin was connected to any of them."

"Can do," Palmer said. "Hey, you want me to write this stuff up in some kind of report? I've got all the case numbers and detectives' names, evidence lists... the whole shooting match."

"No, don't worry about that."

"It's no trouble. I could bang one out tonight and mail it to you tomorrow."

"I don't need any reports. What you've told me is enough for now."

Palmer was quiet for a moment. "Nico, are you working with the police on this?"

"Not exactly."

"You better be careful, pal."

"Just get me the information and don't worry."

"I'll keep all these notes, just in case you change your mind."

"I don't plan on changing my mind. Call me as soon as you get anything."

"I'm on my way out the door, buddy."

SIXTY-SIX

Lenny Pandori set a bottle of wine and three glasses on Anne's kitchen table. Anne filled her glass and went into the living room.

"I can't stand to look at the pictures of those women anymore. And I don't want to hear any more," she said as she walked away.

Nicoletti looked up from the case file folders Pandori had brought back from Billings. He watched his friend struggle to get into the chair on the other side of the table.

"Are you all right?" Nicoletti asked.

"I'm fine. Just a little tired and maybe a little stiff in the joints."

Nicoletti laid out the crime scene photos of the Billings murders. Both female victims were nude, their bodies discovered in a wooded area. They were rolled over on their sides with their knees tucked toward their chests. Their arms were bent at the elbows and their hands were close together below their chins. He rotated the photos and looked at them from several different angles. The painting hidden behind the dresser in Durbin's trophy room flashed in his mind.

"If these victims were kept in the same position and turned upright, with their knees and shins along the ground, they would look like they were praying," Nicoletti said.

Again, he was withholding information from his friend. Again, he felt guilty. He thought of confiding all he knew, all he suspected, and all he planned. But to do so would put Pandori and his career at risk, no matter how things turned out. Especially if the plan failed. No, Nicoletti thought, he must remain silent. He would stick to his plan and act alone.

He turned the photographs toward Pandori and looked him in the eye. "I don't think there is anything here to connect these killings to Marie-Justine's murderer."

"I guess you're right," Pandori said as he flipped through the case files. "The medical examiner's report says both women sustained head wounds prior to death. Marie-Justine wasn't hit in the head."

"Any indication of what caused the injuries?" Nicoletti stopped looking at the photos.

"According to this report, it was a blunt trauma caused by a heavy object approximately twenty millimeters in diameter."

"Twenty millimeters? How big is that?" Nicoletti asked.

"About the thickness of your thumb," Anne said from the other room.

Both men held up their thumbs and examined them. Then Nicoletti thought of Palmer's description: *No big-*

ger than your thumb, but if you snap it just right, you can split a guy's head open like a melon.

"Did the ME note any imprint, like stitching, in the area of the wound?" Nicoletti asked.

Pandori read the documents. "No. They did remove some pale blue nylon fibers from the area of the head wounds and from the hair of both the victims." He looked at Nicoletti. "The police report speculated that the killer threw a blanket over their heads before he hit them." Pandori set the report on the table and picked up his wine glass. "Why do you want to know about stitching?"

"Just asking."

SIXTY-SEVEN

For the third time, Anne protested having to leave her home. "I'm perfectly fine right here."

"No. I don't think you are." Nicoletti crushed a cigarette butt in the terra-cotta planter on the retaining wall adjacent to Anne's back deck. "There is no way to protect you from Durbin while I'm gone."

"Why don't we just go to Garland, tell him what we know and all we suspect, and let the police handle this?"

"We will. But for now, we need to gather a little more information. We have no witness, prints, or DNA." Nicoletti was stalling.

"What more do we need? Durbin knew M-J; he met her twice right here. You saw him touch her hair at the café, and we have his phone calls from the pay phone to her house."

"I saw *someone*, and we have *someone's* calls."

"Someone wearing a gray coat, which you found in his closet."

"I found *a* gray coat."

"The perfume? The duplicate kitchen and bedroom? The painting with the red choker?" Anne's voice grew louder.

"Found by me, during an illegal search."

"So we tell the police and they get a warrant."

"They can't use my information. The defense will argue I was acting as an agent of the police during the break-in. The evidence will be suppressed. We need more." Nicoletti was getting angry with himself. He had more. More than he could stand to think about.

"Durbin was at my house the other night. You followed him home. They could arrest him for trespassing."

"I followed *someone*, probably Durbin, but I can't say for sure. Under cross-examination, I would have to admit it could have been someone else. And if the police grabbed him now for trespassing, he would bond out in an hour. Then he might take off before the cops could build the murder case against him. And if he runs, he'll end up in some unsuspecting town and kill again. I can't allow that."

"You can't allow that? What the hell can you allow? Allow the murderer to stay here, going about his daily business, free to focus on his next victim, who you believe is going to be me?"

She sat on the corner of the wooden coffee table, folded her arms across her chest, and stared at Nicoletti.

"What are you going to do? What's the plan? Why do you have to leave town all of a sudden? Am I supposed to hide in Lenny Pandori's house forever? I have a right to know since I'm the one that fuckin' maniac is after."

"Just give me a few days." He touched her arm. "Let's go over it again, one last time, before I leave for the airport."

"Okay, but you promise to be gone only a few days. Three days at the most."

She stood up and walked back and forth in front of him, like a child reciting the words of a poem she doesn't know the meaning of. "Keep my cell phone fully charged. Carry it with me at all times. You will call me twice a day, starting tomorrow: one call in the morning and another call at night. And even if you don't say a word, I'm to leave the line open for at least three minutes before hanging up."

"And…?"

"And I'm to have no meetings with any friends or go any place where Durbin might see me and follow me back to Pandori's, thereby compromising my safety." She stopped as if waiting for approval.

"And…?"

"And I'm to keep this gun with me at all times—in my waistband, in my purse, or under my pillow—until you get back." She patted the grip of her small revolver that peeked over the top of her braided leather belt.

Nicoletti hugged her. "Just a few more days, I promise."

One hour later, he was on a plane headed for Colorado Springs. He wished Anne were sitting next to him.

SIXTY-EIGHT

Charles Durbin had packed up the Provençal table linens and replaced them with a generic white tablecloth. He had also removed the yellow café curtains and the Vellox tea service. He couldn't take the chance that Jenny Garland had seen the same items in Marie-Justine's kitchen. Now that Jenny was seated at this kitchen table, he was glad he had taken the precautions.

He set a plastic bottle with a sage-green label next to Jenny's wine glass. "Here it is. All you have to do is rub it into your hair, like you would a cream rinse, and let it sit for thirty minutes. Then rinse it out and don't wash your hair again for forty-eight hours."

"Thirty minutes, then forty-eight hours. Got it." Jenny turned the plastic bottle in her hands. "Thank you, Charles. You're terrific."

"I still recommend that you cut your hair short and let it grow out. Keep your natural color for a few months, trim the ends a few times, and you'll be ready to go again." He filled her glass without asking.

"And I still recommend that you rent a riverfront shop and go back into the salon business. You should be using your talents on humans instead of dogs."

"I prefer the dogs."

"I'm serious, Charles. I know everyone in this town. On my recommendations alone, your shop would be packed." She took a long drink of wine. "And think of all the interesting gossip you would hear."

"Speaking of gossip, wasn't that awful about the lady professor they found down by the river? I don't know how your husband can cope with all that horrible business," he said, hoping she would be willing to divulge what she knew.

"It has been tough on him this last week. Tough on both of us."

"Did you know her?"

"Yes, we both did. She was an awesome woman. She lived in that little yellow-and-white cottage over on Elm." Jenny looked directly at Durbin, who gave her a quizzical look. "You remember, I showed it to you when you were thinking of buying an investment property."

"Yes, I remember. I heard the police have a suspect."

"Several, from what Pete says."

"Several? That's a scary thought. The news report said there was only one."

"Pete said they thought they had a good suspect, but they were way off base. The rest of the press releases are just public relations bullshit." She took another drink.

"I also heard there was some criminologist from Washington, DC, helping the police." He put a splash of wine in his own glass to encourage her.

"Oh, that's Joe Nicoletti. He's gone. Left town today."

"For how long?" Durbin's voice was hard.

"I have no idea. Why do you ask?"

"I mean, when will he be coming back to help out on the case?" Durbin softened his voice and added a slight feminine lilt.

"I don't think he's coming back. Seems like everybody's leaving town. I stopped by Anne Bertone's house this morning and she was packing. I guess she's too shook up about Marie-Justine to stay around."

"She's leaving?" He heard the panic in his own voice. "When?"

"Soon. I'd say within the next few days or sooner. Do you know her?" Jenny asked casually.

He almost said no. Then he realized it wouldn't make any sense to be so inquisitive about a stranger. "Yes. I met her a few months ago. She had come by to see about getting a dog." Durbin stopped there. "A very pretty woman, if I remember," he added, just to excite himself.

"Anne and I went to high school together." Jenny was now well on her way to a mild intoxication. She poured more wine.

"Really? I would think she's quite a bit older than you," Durbin lied.

"No, we're the same age."

"I also read in the paper about that elderly professor. That was another tragedy. Fell down the stairs or something. Terrible accident."

"More bullshit." Jenny swallowed a mouthful of wine. "Pete said it wasn't an accident."

"Really? But the paper said—"

"The hell with what the paper said." She leaned forward on the table and lowered her voice. "I probably shouldn't say anything, but Pete thinks Marie-Justine's and Jason Kimba's deaths are connected."

"And why would he think that?" Durbin's voice was barely under control. He was tired of playing with this cow. He wanted to lock his hands around her throat and shake out of her everything she knew.

"I don't know. It was just something he and Joe Nicoletti talked about."

Durbin put a cork in the wine bottle and placed it in the refrigerator before Jenny could refill her glass.

"Sorry to rush off, Jenny, but I've got an appointment on the other side of town in twenty minutes."

He practically pulled her out of the chair, handed her the plastic bottle with the sage label, and waltzed her out the front door before she could say anything more than a quick 'thank-you.'

Durbin paced in front of the painting of the woman with the silver comb in her hair. He had mishandled Jenny Garland, a possible mistake. He might need her again. She didn't like to be pushed, but he'd had to get her out. He needed time to think.

"We're leaving sooner than I thought," he said to the painting. "If they've found a connection between the two murders, I can't imagine what it could be."

Durbin opened the top dresser drawer and lightly touched the silk undergarments. "If we are going to have Anne Bertone, we must take her now."

SIXTY-NINE

From the redwood deck of Ken Palmer's mountainside home, Nicoletti looked down on the shimmering lights of Colorado Springs. Palmer finished his sixth phone call since Nicoletti's arrival.

"That was the last piece of your puzzle, Nico."

Palmer read through several pages of notes as he sat on a lounge chair, a beer bottle between his legs.

"The colonel's daughter took her cat to a veterinary clinic off North Academy Boulevard. Her last appointment was two weeks before she disappeared. Unfortunately, Durbin never worked there."

"Shit. Well, beating the victim didn't fit the pattern, so I guess it was too much to expect. But—"

"Hey, ol' buddy. Calm down now. I said he didn't work there. I didn't say he'd never been there." Palmer waited just long enough for Nicoletti to start to lose his patience. "Durbin had applied for a job there as a dog groomer. The lady vet didn't like him. Said he gave her the creeps. But she took his application anyway and stamped it with a date and time before filing it away."

"Palmer, get to the point." Nicoletti lit a cigarette and dropped the match in his empty beer bottle.

"Hey, can I get you another beer?"

"Fuck you. Now, let's hear it."

"I see you haven't picked up any social graces since your retirement." Palmer pulled one of the papers close to his face, angling it toward the light coming from the living room. "The time stamp puts Durbin at the clinic at one thirty-five in the afternoon. According to the clinic's appointment book, ten minutes later, at one forty-five, the colonel's daughter brought her cat in for a rabies shot."

"He could have easily been in the parking lot, seen her go in, and waited to follow her home." Nicoletti stood up and began to pace along the deck railing.

"That's the way I see it. Not that I want to spoil the moment, but I'm going to need to pay the guy who helped dig all this up for you. He checked out eight clinics between yesterday and today. That's sixteen hours at fifty bucks an hour. You can write the check to my company and I'll pay him."

"I need a gun. One that won't come back to you."

"Nico, I know we've been over this already, but are you sure you want to handle it this way?"

Palmer waited, but Nicoletti did not answer.

"I mean, you know Durbin is your man. And now there's a pretty good chance we can pin him on at least one if not two murders in Colorado."

"Forget it, Palmer. The cops haven't surfaced him as a suspect in any of the murders, and if they screw up and he gets wind of their interest in him, he'll run."

"Yeah, but if they look at all the cases now and focus on Durbin as their only suspect, who knows what they might turn up." Palmer didn't sound very convincing. "And if he runs, so what? They'll catch him."

"And what happens while the cops are trying to figure it out? Do they put Durbin under twenty-four-hour surveillance? For how long? A few weeks? Six months? They don't have the manpower for that, and what they do have doesn't have the experience. And if he burns them and runs, whose daughter or wife will he kill next?"

From a file cabinet in his paneled study, Palmer removed a .45 caliber pistol. He set it on the desk in front of Nicoletti. "This will do the job. It's clean, and when you bring it back, I can change out the barrel and firing pin."

"Too big and too noisy for this job. At night, you can hear a twig snap halfway across this town." Nicoletti did not touch the pistol.

Palmer sighed and reluctantly reached to the back of the filing cabinet. Nicoletti leaned forward as Palmer unwrapped a red flannel cloth to reveal a .22 caliber Beretta, a box of ammunition, and a silencer. "Took this little beauty from a smuggler in Del Rio about twenty years ago. Been saving it for a special occasion. Guess this one is as good as any."

Nicoletti took the flannel package and examined the pistol. "How does it shoot?"

"Within twenty feet it's pretty much dead-on." Palmer returned the .45 to the cabinet and closed the drawer. "You want to try it out?"

"I'll have plenty of time for that along the way."

"Leave it with me tonight. I'll clean it up and oil it. It's been sitting in that drawer for a couple of years. I'll bring it to your hotel in the morning with the box of ammo. When you're done practicing, load the magazine and throw the rest of the ammunition away."

"Got it."

"Nico, if you use it, I never want to see it again. Take it apart and scatter the pieces across hell." Palmer looked at the gun on the table. "I'd really like to have the silencer back if you can manage it."

"I'll also need to borrow your Jeep for a few days. You can keep my rental car until I get back."

"And what am I going to tell my wife when she asks where the Jeep is?"

"Tell her I borrowed it to go camping and fishing. Say I needed to clear my head and you suggested a trip into the mountains." Nicoletti looked around the room. "I'll need to use some of your gear. I won't be staying in any hotels along the way." Nicoletti looked one more time at the small pistol. "Now, don't forget—"

"I know, call the lady reporter twice a day: once in the morning, by nine, from your hotel room phone; and again at night, around ten, from your cell phone."

"Her name is Anne."

"Does she know what you're up to?"

"No. And she isn't going to."

"Remember, Nico, they said this Durbin was quick and strong."

"Relax, old man. I've no intention of turning this into a wrestling match."

SEVENTY

Nicoletti woke to the phone ringing. The hotel room was black. For a few seconds, he didn't know where he was. The clock on the radio told him it was ten minutes after twelve. The phone rang again.

"Nico, it's me." Pandori sounded wide-awake. "Anne gave me your hotel number."

"What's wrong?" Nicoletti asked as he regained his bearings. "Is she all right?"

"She's fine, asleep in the guest room. I just wanted to run something by you."

"At midnight?" Nicoletti turned on the bedside light.

"Reichert developed those photos I told you about, the ones from that grad student, Sommer. He wants you to take a look at them when you get back. He wants to see if you recognize any of the people in the background of some of the shots."

"Did you tell him anything about Durbin?"

"No. I haven't told them anything. I told you I'd wait until you thought there was enough to list Durbin as a solid suspect." Pandori breathed heavily. "I know what you're doing, Nico. I knew you were headed this way from the start. To tell you the truth, I was hoping you might change your mind, but I know you haven't."

"Lenny, I'm not doing anything. I just came to Colorado Springs for a couple of days to check out a few leads and—"

"Don't bullshit me, Nico. I know what's up. Yesterday, when we were going over the files of the Billings murders, you didn't ask me one real question about the cases. That's when I knew you'd already decided to handle this your way."

"And what if I have? Are you going to try and stop me, or have Reichert and Garland jump in the middle of this?"

"No. I just wanted you to know that when the time comes, if you need me, I'll be there." Pandori's breathing sounded labored.

"Are you having a heart attack? It sounds like you're gasping your last breath."

"I'm lighting a cigar, asshole." Pandori let out an extended exhale. "And since you never asked, and since you're in Colorado Springs, I thought I'd give you a little more to check out."

"Am I going to need a pencil?" Nicoletti opened the nightstand drawer and picked up a pad and a pen.

"The first victim, Lisa Waterford, was a Canadian tourist from Toronto. I was going through the evidence list of the stuff they found in her Missoula hotel room." The sound of Pandori puffing on his cigar was so loud, Nicoletti thought he could smell the smoke. "In one of her suitcases were two matchbooks and a receipt from the Broadmoor Hotel. It's—"

"I know the place. When was she there?" Nicoletti poised the pen over the pad.

"The receipt is from the hotel gift shop. The date is February eighth of this year."

"Did she stay there?"

"The cops never looked into it. When I saw it on the list, I figured you could check it out since you're down there." More puffing. "So what have you got, other than an old driver's license that ties Durbin to Colorado Springs?"

"I'm not sure. I've got a few days of checking out some leads. I'll fill you in when I get back."

"Well, see if you can tie him to the Broadmoor last winter and—"

"I'll handle it," Nicoletti cut him off. He leaned back and propped himself on the extra pillows. "You know how when you're out in the ocean and you see storm clouds starting to gather? You can either brace yourself for the hit or you can try to outrun it."

"Your point?"

"Well, I was just thinking... It seems that in my life, all the really turbulent jolts came out of the blue. No warning, no chance to brace myself. Just... wham."

"Get some sleep, Nico." Pandori's voice was softer.

"Hey, why did you call my room? Why not my cell?"

"I just wanted to see if you were really in a hotel in Colorado Springs and not just using it as a flimsy alibi while you slipped through Durbin's back door."

SEVENTY-ONE

At five in the morning, Ken Palmer arrived in front of the hotel. He handed a car key to Nicoletti.

"The Jeep has a full tank. The camping gear is stowed in the back."

Nicoletti picked up a black bag from the front passenger seat. Inside the bag were the pistol and ammunition, wrapped in the red flannel cloth.

Palmer pulled a couple of pairs of thin, green plastic gloves from his coat pocket. "Bought a box of these last summer to wear when I stained my deck. Never got the deck done. Thought you could use them when you handle the weapon." Palmer held up a cell phone. "You've got a hundred dollars worth of calls on it, just in case of emergency. I've got another one just like it. Here's my number. Don't worry, they're both untraceable."

At ten o'clock, a few miles from the interstate, Nicoletti stopped at a small general store north of Cheyenne. He dialed the cell number Palmer had given him from a pay phone and deposited the exact change.

"Everything go okay?" he asked Palmer.

"What do you think? I'm too old to be trusted? Hey, I didn't say anything on the phone, but your friend Anne carried on quite the one-sided conversation. She's got a real sexy voice."

"I'll check with you later." Nicoletti pictured Anne standing in her living room, wearing her low-cut black dress, tan and firm, the muscular curves of her legs, the late-day sun filtering through the window, warming her body. *We're going out for dinner like civilized people,* she had said to him.

Two hours later, Nicoletti pulled off the highway and found a dirt road that led to nowhere. He parked the Jeep next to a never-ending fence line. From a paper bag full of items he had purchased at a grocery before leaving Colorado Springs, he took an apple and a skull-sized pumpkin. He walked away from the Jeep and set the pumpkin on top of a fence post. A few yards further on, he set the apple on another post.

He held the gun out to his right, as far from his body as he could, just in case it blew up in his hand. He fired the first two rounds without the silencer. The next two, with the silencer screwed into the end of the barrel, made no more noise than a hand slapping against a pillow.

The plastic gloves didn't slip. He missed the apple twice. Hitting the pumpkin was no problem. After each shot, he watched the extracted brass casings spit to the right, no more than two feet away. That would make their recovery easy after Durbin was down. He threw the damaged pumpkin into the field behind the fence and reloaded the pistol before taking off the gloves.

As he drove onto the highway, he took a bite of the apple. *Yeah, I'm just like civilized people,* he thought.

SEVENTY-TWO

Parked in the driveway, Anne Bertone looked at her house. It was dark, inside and out. She hesitated to get out of her car. Maybe she should have waited for Pandori to get home. He could have sat in the car, or gone with her into the house, while she gathered her research notes. Pandori was going to be really pissed when he got home and found her message.

If she hurried, she could get her notes and some more clothes and get back to Pandori's before he did. Then he would be none the wiser. "Speaking of wiser," she said aloud, "you should have gotten over here before dark."

She slung her large leather purse over her head so that it fell under her right arm. She pressed against the leather until she felt the revolver, secure in a zipped inside pocket. "Get going, you wimp," she said as she stepped from the car and headed for the front door.

Anne didn't want to turn on the lights. Suppose that freak Durbin was driving by. If he saw a light, he might start peeking in the windows—or worse. Still, walking around the house in the dark was just stupid. She flicked on a small lamp in the living room.

First she gathered her notes from the kitchen table, the desk, and from on top of the refrigerator. She looked around for other stacks of paper. "I really must get organized," she mumbled as she grabbed two packs of cigarettes from a kitchen cabinet, dropped them in her purse, and zipped it shut.

She struggled a little in the bedroom, holding the notes under her left arm while digging through her dresser for a few clean clothes.

She was partially bent over, squinting to see in the dimly lit drawer, when the blanket was thrown over her head. At first she thought the light in the living room had gone out. Then she felt the blanket against her face. She started to straighten up and scream, but she never made a sound. The blow to her head came too quickly.

SEVENTY-THREE

A few miles outside the city of Missoula, Nicoletti pulled to the side of the road. His plan was simple. Once he was sure Durbin was home and alone, he would go to the front door, identify himself, and hand Durbin his identification case. While Durbin examined the credentials and badge, Nicoletti would raise the silenced pistol and fire the first round into Durbin's eye. If necessary, he would fire again. If it was necessary.

That scenario had been set in Nicoletti's mind since he got on the elevator in his Colorado Springs hotel. Prior to that, he had planned to follow Durbin around town until the right opportunity presented itself.

For the several hours and hundreds of miles, Nicoletti had not thought about killing Durbin. Instead, he had argued in his head, and occasionally out loud, with Anne, Pandori, and Palmer. Each of them had, in their own way, asked him to reconsider his course of action. They asked him to rely on the law, on the police investigation, on the evidence in hand and the evidence to come. He had rejected their suggestions, acting as if they did not fully comprehend the mission—that only he knew the truth and only he could make things right. Now he had to convince himself.

Sitting on the side of the highway in the dark, a wet snow falling on the windshield, he was only a few minutes from completing that mission. But completing it for whom? At first he thought it was for Marie-Justine—to avenge her death and punish her killer. Then he thought maybe it was what he had told Anne and Palmer—to keep Durbin from killing again.

But somewhere in the last few miles, it occurred to him that he was doing it for himself. To show God, or fate, that he wasn't going to stand by and take it. "No more reaching into my life and fucking with it," he had said above the music from the car radio.

The cell phone rang. Only Palmer knew the number.

"Nico, I just picked up a message from your voicemail at the hotel," Palmer said. "It was from your friend Lenny. He said Anne wasn't home when he got there. She left him a note that said she'd be back at six. She's still not there."

"When did he leave the message?"

"Just a few minutes ago. The phone was ringing when I got to your room."

Nicoletti disconnected and dialed Pandori's cell phone.

"Have you found her?" Nicoletti asked as he pulled the Jeep back onto the highway.

"I'm headed to her house right now. She's not answering her cell phone," Pandori said.

"Call me as soon as you get there. I'm about ten minutes away."

"I thought you were in Colorado."

"Call me."

Nicoletti accelerated. He felt the Jeep's tires start to lose contact with the wet road. Then he realized Pandori did not know the number of the phone Palmer had given him. He dialed Pandori again.

"I'm just pulling up. Her car is in the driveway. There's a light on inside. Hold on."

He could hear the wind and Pandori walking and grunting.

"The front door is unlocked."

The sound of the wind stopped. Heavy breathing. Footsteps. Pandori was inside.

"Nothing, Nico. No one's here. The back door is wide open. There are her notes scattered all over the floor."

"Meet me at Durbin's. I'm five minutes away. If his gray Suburban is behind the house, pull in at the north end of the alley to block him in. I'll park at the south."

"I'm on my way."

"Lenny," Nicoletti said quietly, "don't go near the house without me. And if Durbin gets near you, don't be a hero."

"Nico, I got a phone in one hand, a cane in the other, and somewhere in between I'm trying to figure out how to hold a gun. Don't worry. I'll save all the hero shit for you. See you in five."

SEVENTY-FOUR

Nicoletti drove past the front of the house. There was a light in the upstairs bedroom, Durbin's room. He pulled the Jeep into the alley, killed the headlights, and rolled to a stop. The Suburban was backed in against the house. The snow was sticking to the roof but had melted on the windshield and the hood. It hadn't been there long.

He walked quickly to Pandori's car. It was angled to block the other end of the alley. Pandori wasn't inside.

Nicoletti ran back to the house. One set of footprints in the snow led to the right side of the house. The basement door was ajar. Carefully, he eased his way down the stone steps and across the musty room. A dim light spread across the steps leading up to the kitchen. He saw Pandori's cane leaning against the stair rail.

"I told you to wait," Nicoletti whispered to himself. He drew the silenced pistol from his waistband and started up the steps to the kitchen.

He was at the top step before he saw the boots—men's boots—then the legs, then the blood. A lot of blood.

Lenny was partially rolled onto his side. He looked at Nicoletti and raised a finger to his lips. Nicoletti moved closer. Pandori moved the finger and pointed up to the second floor.

Nicoletti nodded and started to reach for his friend. Pandori's jacket was open, the blood soaking through his shirt and smearing on the floor with every move he made. Nicoletti touched the face of his wounded friend.

"He was too fast. He's got my gun." He laid his head against the floor. "I'm sorry, Nico."

Quietly, he started up the polished wooden stairs. Light came from the open bedroom door. Nicoletti noticed a line of light at the bottom of the closed door on his left. He remembered the door opened into the bathroom that connected to Durbin's bedroom. He thought about yanking open the bathroom door. He reached for it but realized if it was locked from the inside, he'd lose the element of surprise. He pulled his arm back and moved toward the open bedroom door.

He knew he was making too much noise. The sound of the blood pounding in his ears and chest was enough to give him away. He crouched slightly, his arms fully extended in front of him, a two-handed grip on the gun. When the barrel of the gun reached the door jamb, he stopped. He balanced himself on the balls of his feet and gradually moved to his right, always looking over the front sight of the pistol.

Durbin's bedroom revealed itself to Nicoletti in small slices. On top of the dresser, he could see Pandori's 9mm pistol. At least Durbin wasn't holding it. He moved to his right, half step by half step. He listened but heard nothing. He took another half step. He heard a noise, a woman's groan.

A half step more and he saw Anne, her mouth gagged with a black cloth, her arms and legs outstretched, each tied to one of the four heavy wooden bedposts. She was in a red silk dress with golden dragons clawing across her shoulders. Her hair was pulled to the side and held with a silver comb. A red choker was tied around her neck. Nicoletti knew she was the living version of the painting hanging on the wall across the hall.

She saw him. Her eyes closed for a moment, then opened wide and looked in the direction of the bath-room. Nicoletti shifted his weight and entered the room. He stepped left, moving along the wall. Light escaped from around the partially closed bathroom door. He moved toward it and stopped to listen.

Anne let out a muffled scream. Nicoletti turned in time to see something large and dark, cutting through the air above his head. As it started to envelope him, he realized it was a blanket. He turned to his left but was stopped by the wall. Spinning to his right, he crouched low as the blanket began to fall. He instinctively ducked his head and raised his left arm.

Durbin's first blow struck somewhere between Nico-letti's left shoulder and bicep. The impact sent a spike of pain up his arm and into his neck. The blows continued in rapid succession.

Nicoletti stopped thinking. Instinctively, he kept turning into the blanket, hoping to get far enough under it to come out the other side.

He swung his damaged left arm over his head. The blanket wrapped around it. As his arm lowered, it pulled part of the shroud behind him. He could see a pair of boots in front of him.

From under the edge of the blanket, he fired three rounds: once into the boot, then a shin, then a thigh. The blanket was gone.

Charles Durbin stood before him, a blackjack in his left hand and a large combat knife in his right.

Nicoletti fired again, stomach, again, chest. Durbin fell forward onto his knees and his arms hung at his sides. He looked Nicoletti in the eye, then at the end of the silencer. His head lowered until his chin rested on his chest.

Nicoletti pointed the pistol at the center of Durbin's skull. He lowered the barrel and lashed out with his left leg, smashing his boot into the right side of Durbin's face. The killer spun on his knees, dropped the knife and the leather blackjack, and fell against the wall.

Nicoletti kicked the knife and blackjack across the room. He nudged his boot against Durbin's head. There was no response, but he was still breathing.

Anne was tied with nylon dog leashes. He freed her hands, leaving the gag and the legs to her. He took a leash from the bed and bound Durbin's arms securely behind his back. He used a second leash to tie Durbin's ankles together.

A crashing sound came from below.

"Lenny."

Nicoletti ran from the room into the hall.

SEVENTY-FIVE

At the bottom of the staircase, Nicoletti was met by Chief Garland and Detective Reichert.

"Pandori," Nicoletti said.

"Paramedics got him," Garland said. "Where's Durbin?"

"Upstairs. Alive. How did you know where we were?"

"Pandori called me at home," Garland said. "Gave me the address and told me to bring an ambulance."

A single gunshot roared from above. The three men scrambled up the stairs. They burst into the bedroom, guns drawn.

Anne was standing over Durbin's body, his hands and feet still bound. In her left hand was her brown leather purse. In her right, she held her gun.

She stood motionless, staring at Durbin.

From inside the doorway, Nicoletti saw the back of Durbin's head, blood smeared on the wall with a matting of hair, bone fragments, and brain matter.

"Anne, it's all right," Garland said calmly as he slowly approached her. He repeated the phrase several times as he touched her right shoulder and slid his hand down her arm until her gun was firmly in his hand. "Everything is all right, Anne. Give me the gun."

Anne released her grip on the weapon and looked at Nicoletti.

Garland slid the revolver into his coat pocket and nudged Anne in Nicoletti's direction.

Reichert knelt at the side of the body and placed two fingers against Durbin's twisted neck.

"Dead." Reichert wiped his fingers along the side of his pant leg and spoke directly to Garland.

Nicoletti took Anne into his arms and held her as she placed the side of her head against his chest. From his right hand dangled the silenced pistol. Nicoletti watched Garland take Lenny Pandori's pistol from the top of the dresser.

"Untie his hands," Garland said to Reichert.

"Shouldn't we get some pictures of this first?" Reichert asked.

"Untie his hands," Garland repeated. He looked at Nicoletti, then around the room at the bed, the dog leads tied to the sturdy wooden posts, the knife and blackjack on the floor at the edge of the bed. He looked back at Nicoletti.

Nicoletti nodded in approval of the unspoken plan.

"Pull his arms in front of him," Garland ordered Reichert, "and put this in his right hand." He handed Pandori's pistol to the kneeling detective. "It was self-defense."

"But Chief—" Reichert began.

"I said self-defense. Now, make it happen." Garland sat on the edge of the bed, watching Reichert. He looked again at Nicoletti. "Take Anne down to my office. I'll meet you there once we're done here." Garland pulled a radio from his belt. "I'll tell the duty sergeant to let you wait in my office 'til I get there."

Nicoletti guided Anne with his left hand, turning her so she could not see Durbin's body.

"Nico," Garland said. "There's a bottle of scotch in the lower-left drawer of my desk."

SEVENTY-SIX

For six days, the wind had blown from the north across the French countryside. For six days, Nicoletti had been cold. His left shoulder, knee, and hip ached. The only respite from the cold had come in the late afternoons and evenings when he sat near the fire with Marie-Justine's grandfather and Anne Bertone. If they had been suffering from the cold, they never said. Instead, their days seemed to be filled with laughter and kindness as they went about the daily chores.

Sometime during the night, the wind had stopped. The January sun had found the strength to burn off the morning fog. It heated his shoulders and back as he stood next to the small hilltop cemetery. At his feet, the massive male Great Pyrenees stretched in the pale light, never averting its eyes from the house.

Ten minutes earlier, a well-dressed middle-aged man had arrived in a highly polished black Peugeot sedan. Now the man stood in the driveway in animated conversation, separated from Grand-père and Anne by the female Pyrenees, who acted as an immoveable barrier between them.

The Peugeot departed. Grand-père Joseph went into the house, followed by both dogs. Anne walked toward Nicoletti.

"What was that all about?" he asked.

"He was an estate agent with British buyers. They are looking for a vacation home with a vineyard, and, I might add, are willing to pay an exorbitant sum."

"What did the old man say?"

"He told him he already had someone to take over the property." She placed her arm inside his and moved him along the gravel walkway.

"I wasn't aware he was planning on giving up his home."

"He's not. He said the new owner is going to allow him to continue living here until God calls him."

"Who is this new owner?"

"Don't know. He said it was someone who would tend the garden and the vineyard. Someone he's going to teach to make wine. Someone who would respect the family cemetery."

Nicoletti was quiet as he looked across the hillside vineyard.

"Have you reconsidered leaving with me tomorrow?" she asked.

"Have you considered staying a while longer?" He hugged her. "What will I do without my personal interpreter?"

"I have to get back. I have too much to do back home." She pulled away from his side. "Seriously, Nico, how long before the real world drags you back?"

"I'm not ready to go back."

"And I'm not ready to stay."

They walked a bit farther before turning back toward the house.

"He's arranged for all of us to have dinner at his favorite restaurant tonight," she said.

"Why? I thought we'd agreed I'd cook."

"He has planned it as a little farewell celebration for me, and he wants to introduce you to other grape growers in the valley."

From the vineyard, Grand-père Joseph called out to them. He was waving a bottle of wine and carrying glasses.

Nicoletti waved. "What is he saying?"

"He said he has something he wants to teach you about the vines."

"Let's go," he said, pulling her hand.

"You go. I'm going back to the house for a while."

"Come on, please."

"Nico, he wants to talk to you. He's only carrying two glasses."

THE END

Also by Laurence Giliotti

GAMBRELLI AND THE PROSECUTOR

It is September, 1934. On a French coastal island, the Provincial Police arrest the senior prosecutor in the Ministry of Justice for the murder of his mistress. Chief Inspector Gambrelli, of the Metropolitan Police, is dispatched from the city to review the case and report his findings to the Ministry.

Suffering the heat and humidity of the island, Gambrelli begins his inquiry asking more questions than the local authorities can answer. He leaves the sun-bleached, sandy streets of the island and returns to the grand boulevards and cobblestone alleyways of the city. Methodically, he probes the lives of the prosecutor, his wife, and his mistress. Simultaneously, detectives search the city for the murdered woman's younger sister, fearing she may become the killer's next victim.

Following a twisting path of love, betrayal, greed and violence, Gambrelli searches for the motive that led a killer to a young woman's door.

Acclaim for

GAMBRELLI AND THE PROSECUTOR

"*Gambrelli and the Prosecutor* is a wonderful, absorbing debut novel from newcomer Laurence Giliotti. Set in the 1930s, this well-crafted procedural is fast-paced and exciting while exuding a strong—almost nostalgic—love for the sandwich years between the two world wars."

"If you are a huge Georges Simenon fan or merely a casual mystery reader with a hankering for a twist of European flavor in your police procedurals, you must read this little known gem...in what deserves to be a best-selling series."
—San Francisco Book Review

"The spirit of Georges Simenon is alive and well in this novel."

"...a compelling story...vivid cast of characters."

"Gambrelli is a wonderful personality, a civilized man doing an uncivilized job as best he can."

"Gambrelli and his crew are such a delight that readers will hope the author is diligently at work on a sequel."
—Kirkus Reviews

"...a thrilling story full of suspense..."

"...Gambrelli is sure to win over readers and get them hooked on what promises to be an exciting series..."

"The book reads as if it is a series that has been ongoing for some time, but readers will find a delightful surprise to discover *Gambrelli and the Prosecutor* is only the beginning."
—Portland Book Review

Forthcoming from
Château Noir Publishing in 2016...

GAMBRELLI AND THE BANKERS

France, October, 1934. Germany's Deputy Minister of Finance falls to his death from the balcony of his hotel room in an apparent suicide. He is the fourth prominent German to meet a violent death within the jurisdiction of the Metropolitan Police in the last three months.

The same evening, the patriarch of France's wealthiest banking family dies in his sleep, the unfortunate victim of an accidental gas leak.

Both cases are assigned to the Major Crimes Bureau with instructions to resolve the official inquiries as quickly and discreetly as possible. A simple matter. All Chief Inspector Gambrelli has to do is sign the preliminary reports: a suicide and an accident.

Gambrelli hesitates. Nothing is ever as simple as it seems.

Made in the USA
San Bernardino, CA
07 March 2017

46474833R00171